EARLY PRAISE FOR CHANCE TO FADE & OTHER STORIES

"Josh Rank shows a boundless, tender understanding of the small anxieties that loom large enough to consume us. The stories in Chance to Fade are centered around a heartbreaking question: who could we be to each other if we could see each other true? Rank shows us his answer, and in this way, we're a little bit closer to our own. These stories are gems."

~ Zach VandeZande, author of *Liminal Domestic* and *Lesser American Boys*

"The stories in Josh Rank's *Chance to Fade & Other Stories* do exactly what good fiction is supposed to do: engage, entertain, challenge, and surprise. Rank excels at creating compelling characters, putting them in unique situations, and letting the sparks fly. The centerpiece is the novella-length title story, in which all of the author's talents shine. Put *Chance to Fade & Other Stories* on your list of must-read books."

~ Chuck Augello, Contributing Editor, *Cease Cows* and author of *The Revolving Heart* and *Talking Vonnegut: Centennial Interviews and Essays*

"Josh Rank's *Chance to Fade and Other Stories* is a breathtaking exploration of the ways luck and chance affect our lives. The characters in these stories are real and broken and searching for answers in an unforgiving world in which they're also looking for agency, control. On the flipside of that equation, Rank has complete control of his craft in this collection. There aren't two stories here that function the same way. Each piece presents unique perspectives, structures, voices, and most importantly, ways to punch the reader in the gut. Sprinkled with beautifully speculative weirdness in all the right ways, *Chance to Fade* is at once familiar and surprising, and I had to force myself to savor Rank's language, lest I blaze through the collection in one sitting."

~ Cody Shrum,
Identity Theory Fiction Editor and Author of *Green Acre*

"Rank is a master at finding stories in that difficult-to-locate space between mundanity and magic, where everything feels both familiar and unsettling. I found this collection very moving, fun, and consistently surprising. A wonderful book."

~ Mike Nagel,
author of *Duplex* and *Culdesac*

JOSH RANK

Chance to Fade & Other Stories

*For Alameda,
my continual inspiration.*

CONTENTS

Major Release … 9

Earplugs … 13

Patio … 31

The Rain … 35

Near the Tree Line … 43

Scratch Off … 47

I Collect Teeth … 63

Drowning Without Sinking … 67

The Truth … 71

Lucky … 75

Feathers … 87

Fireworks … 91

Hopi … 113

Rachel + Jeremy … 117

Chance to Fade … 127

MAJOR RELEASE

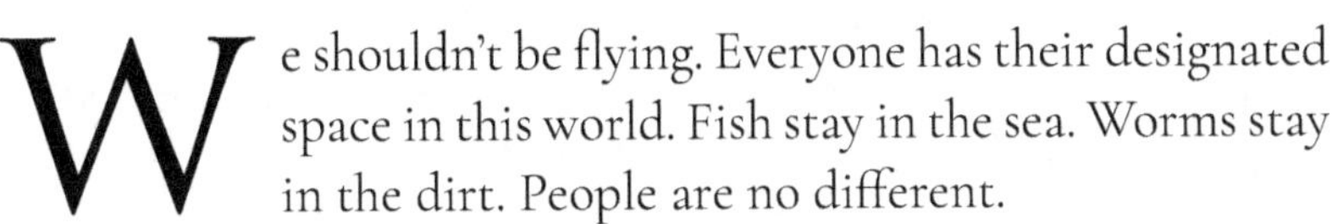

We shouldn't be flying. Everyone has their designated space in this world. Fish stay in the sea. Worms stay in the dirt. People are no different.

I told her this, sitting in seat A row 17. The window seat. She sat in seat B.

The horizon stretched beyond the fields of what I guessed was Oklahoma. All I knew was that it was flat and there was another hour or two until we landed in Atlanta.

"Why would you say that?" she asked.

She was one of those people that truly believed the world could change. That people could change. There was nothing somebody couldn't overcome with the right amount of moxie and determination.

And I believed people shouldn't be in the sky.

Connections don't have to make sense. I can't explain how an outlet connects to a lightbulb within a lamp, but I know what happens when you flip the switch after plugging it in. And that's what happened with us. We were plugged in. Maybe it was the fact that both of us had to stay in Atlanta for three nights and didn't know anybody besides coworkers. Maybe the fact that we were staying in the same part of town helped out.

We traded numbers as we taxied toward our gate and ended up getting chicken wings later that night from some place she saw on TV.

Looking back, there are some experiences that have a different sheen to them. Certain memories feel more shiny in some way, like they were treated with an extra filter by a post-production crew. I liked to think it's like comparing the quality of a daytime soap opera to a major release in theaters. But then again, that was my industry. Maybe it was just a way to interpret my stupid ideas through my own prism.

Two full days and three nights. The mornings and afternoons were spent making sure the sets I designed met the needs of the director and then I'd be free at night. She spent her days in business casual attire attending lectures and presentations about new medical devices.

New cities are great ways to separate normal life and the extra sheen. Vacation is one thing. That's planned. But a work trip turning into a major release was a surprise.

We sat at the bar on the top floor of a hotel where neither of us had a room. It spun slowly, very slowly, to show off the surrounding cityscape. She ordered a Manhattan, and me a Pabst.

"Do you ever think about the past?" she asked me. "All the time."

She sipped her drink slowly, as if she didn't actually like it. "What a waste."

The lights of a plane blinked their way out of a cloud to the north, slowly making its way to the airport.

Context has a lot to do with our interactions. A phrase or expression might fit perfectly at the top of a ferris wheel but can get you fired in the boardroom. We understand this when it comes to a work environment, but for some reason it gets muddled in social situations.

For instance, I asked her that night if she'd ever gone skydiving. She said no, not yet.

Then a month later back in LA I asked her the same thing. She rolled her eyes and walked out of the bedroom.

The only difference was context. One had the sheen of a major release, the other had the quick turnaround of a daytime soap opera.

What's more important, quantity or quality?

The last night in Atlanta, I had already forgotten how the shoot went that day. We met on the corner of Peachtree Street and Peachtree Plaza.

"Does every street have the same name around here?" she asked as we looked up at the intersecting street signs.

"Let's find out," I said and we started walking north.

We shouldn't have been there. Not earlier, in the sky and not now, in the city. People are meant to stay on the earth. And if they want to travel, it should be done on the ground. Moving from one side of the country to the other in a matter of hours discombobulates your senses. We might as well have been drunk for the two full days and three nights we baked in the constant humidity.

A week later, we'd be back in Los Angeles. She'd spend her days in the office and I'd be at the studio. The travel buzz would be gone and we'd find out in another month or so that whatever had plugged us in on the flight to Atlanta was born of convenience.

Finally one day outside of her apartment complex, sitting on the concrete stairs framed by two massive palm trees, she looked at me and told me I was right about flying, but not completely.

"What does that mean?" I asked.

"Fish stay in the sea. Worms stay in the dirt."

I walked to the bus stop that night knowing I wouldn't be back.

I still fly. And I'm sure she does, too. Knowing we have no business in the sky isn't going to keep people from bursting out of clouds, wing lights blinking against the unsuspecting, thin air.

EARPLUGS

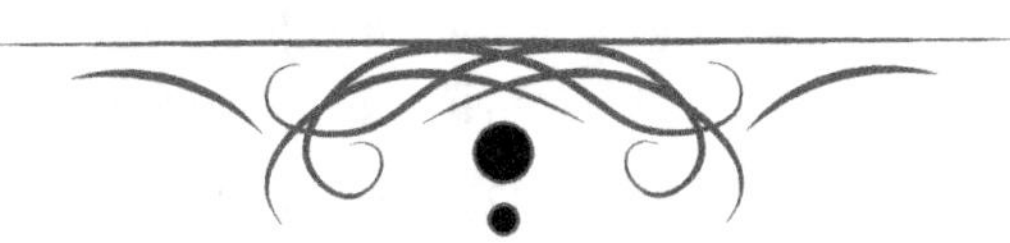

The phones didn't really ring. They weren't really phones, when you got down to it. It was a room full of people wearing headsets and clicking away on their computers between calls. Some days were busy. Calls coming in back-to-back. More often, no one was having troubles, leaving the lines open and allowing coworkers the opportunity to look at the person next to them and say: "We're going to a bar tonight for Susan's birthday."

John looked at the man sitting at the computer next to him, mid-twenties, sloppily tucked-in t-shirt, uncombed hair. His name was Ben. The familiar flash of nervousness pulsed through John's body, as tended to happen when he realized a sentence was directed at him.

"I, uh—" John put his hands under his thighs and looked toward the ceiling just above his coworker's head. How many excuses had he used up to this point? How many times had he repeated them? Luckily, his headset beeped and a message window appeared on his screen. John held up a finger to the uncombed man sitting next to him.

"Thank you for calling Zinc, this is John, how can I help you?" Ride-sharing apps had demolished the taxi service, but that didn't mean there weren't occasional hiccups. People will always have problems with people, and that's where John and his coworkers came in. The days were filled with assuaging fear, agreeing with gripes, and at its base, bolstering self-esteem.

Mostly, he offered credits for free rides until the caller calmed down.

Six more calls and three more awkward conversations later, John clicked the *Pause* button on his computer monitor and stood up. Ben groaned as he stretched and again looked toward John. "I'm going to get you to get a burger with me one of these days," he said with a smile.

John shrugged and kept his eyes on the floor. His heart raced. He wanted nothing more than to open the plastic grocery bag sitting in the refrigerator in the break room and eat quietly in the corner.

"Alright, I know. Same thing every day." Ben gave John a light pat on the shoulder which sent another shockwave through his body. He wasn't used to physical contact, no matter how brief or casual. John walked down the aisle past the rows of computers until he reached the gymnasium-style doors at the end. He had seen too many people lick Cheeto dust from their fingers and grasp the horizontal bar in the middle on their way to the bathroom. At best, he would time his exit with another person. At worst, he would back into it and exit the room looking behind him like a bank robber covering the guards on his way out. Today, the door began to swing open before this became an issue.

"Hey John," she said as she opened the door with her foot. Susan held a box in her hands and smiled that beautiful smile over the top of it. She had only worked there for a month, but was already one of the stars. He mumbled a hello and tried to catch the door before it shut behind her. She didn't move far enough out of the way.

"I know it's kinda dumb to bring your own birthday cake, but that's the world we live in. If you like stuff that doesn't suck, it'll be in the break room. Hurry before Andy eats it all." A middle finger shot up from behind a monitor four rows back.

John didn't have trouble avoiding the door as the stampede followed the box of cake. He sighed as he watched the break room, normally empty due to the plethora of restaurants surrounding their building, fill up. He opened the refrigerator and grabbed the lunch he put together even though he was fifteen minutes late that morning.

"John? Everyone likes vanilla."

He turned around and saw that award-winning smile. She held a paper plate with a slice of cake to him.

"I, uh—" He nodded his head toward the plastic bag hanging from his hand.

"People say vanilla is boring because they think of it as plain. But it's not plain. It's vanilla and vanilla is delicious."

John knew she was right. He looked at the cake and swallowed the saliva building in his mouth. He shook his head.

"I better not," he said. He walked out of the break room, took the elevator downstairs, and ate his lunch standing up because the only bench he could see was at the bus stop.

The afternoon slid by as awkwardly as his reentry to the workspace. His coworkers were unflinchingly kind no matter how many times he refused their offers. The hydraulic of his rolling chair squeaked when he sat down and Ben gave him a brief nod of recognition. John wished he could have asked Ben how his lunch was. Or offered to take him out after work. Or simply patted him on the shoulder as he walked past, but he couldn't.

The afternoon sun finally started to peek through the small window behind John, which at this time of year meant it was about time to go home. He finished his last call—someone had lost their wallet in the car—and logged out of the company's system.

He followed a tall woman he had never spoken to in order to avoid the bar on the door when, again, Susan came through the opposite side.

"Hey, Becky! Oh and John. Good. Listen, it sounds like Gary and the guys are dragging me out to Duke's up the road for a pitcher or twenty of beer. I promise I'll only ask you to sing the birthday song ten or fifteen times. You in?"

The woman in front of John seemed to be nodding her head while he scrambled for an excuse.

"John?" Susan gave him her full attention, and it made him feel like he was melting.

"I, uh—" He glanced around the office and hoped for an earthquake, or a terrorist attack, or a meteor impact, but the only rumbling was beneath his ribcage. "I gotta water my plants."

If she weren't looking him in the face, he would have bit a hole in his tongue.

"Oh." She almost laughed and then her smile faded a few degrees. "Okay, John."

"Have fun," he said quickly and then dodged around her and caught the door with his foot.

Twenty minutes later, the doorknob to his one bedroom apartment felt colder than usual.

He fell into his nightly habit of kicking himself for the way the wrong words seemed to form themselves. He ate a simple dinner of baked chicken breast with instant mashed potatoes and a glass of water, and watched the sunlight fade from the walls.

He could hear his neighbors nearly all the time. They weren't loud. The walls were paper thin. He didn't mind. The illusion of company was nice and he didn't have to worry about them waking him up in the middle of the night. The earplugs took care of that.

Bugs had always been a source of anxiety. It only took one scene in a TV show a few years before where a centipede crawled into a sleeping character's ear to keep John awake at night. He bought some earplugs to dam them out, ensuring he would miss his alarm at least a few times a week. Luckily his manager had a soft spot for him and rarely seemed angry when John would scramble in fifteen minutes or a half hour after his scheduled time.

As soon as the dishes were done and the sun was almost gone, he walked to the cabinet and shook a few sleeping pills into his palm. He tossed the empty bottle into the trashcan in the bathroom. He studied the blue label and made a mental note to avoid buying the same brand the next time he went to the store. A few years of experimenting with various sleeping pills had brought his tolerance to indefensible levels. He swallowed the pills with a sip of water and rolled the earplugs between his thumb and forefinger as he walked into his bedroom. The sun had set but the sky remained a vague orange above the horizon.

Each morning started with a grasp at the notebook next to his bed. He scribbled frantically with his pen to race the fading memory of his dreams. Lucid dreaming had taken a while to get used to, but there were tricks. The main problem after realizing you were in a dream was to keep your excitement in check and avoid waking yourself up. But again, it just took practice. As soon as he chronicled the dreamscapes and alternate realities where he could look people in the eye and speak without his mouth's filter, he would look at the clock and see if he had woken up before or after his alarm. The earplugs made the alarm mostly pointless, but he felt the need to at least try. Failing after an attempt was different than deciding to fail beforehand.

Today, as would occasionally happen, he woke up early and took the time to make breakfast before putting together his lunch.

The office was mostly quiet, a little more serene, when he showed up on time. This morning, the sky was clear but the sunshine had yet to fully take hold of the atmosphere. He sat down at his computer and flicked it on.

A few minutes later, Ben sat down next to him. "You missed it, man."

John had a few theories as to why his coworkers were unendingly inclusive. Most were based on the abused puppy scenario. John's uncle promised his children a dog one Christmas, but waited until finding "the perfect one." This probably meant any dog he could get for free, and in this case, he got what he paid for.

The dog was a beautiful two-year-old beagle named Alameda, but no one could account for the first two years. She had been found on the side of the road after a frenzied foot chase.

Alameda wasn't aggressive, but she wasn't particularly friendly, either. She spent most of her time running from room to room, avoiding groups of people, and shaking in a corner when she couldn't. Her heartbreaking feebleness had an endearing quality to it, and people couldn't help but to root for her. Any show of affection, no matter how tiny, was celebrated. He was the office's Alameda, and couldn't decide if that was okay with him.

"I think we sang happy birthday about fifty times." Ben flicked on his computer and leaned back in his chair. "I almost pulled a you and slept through my alarm today."

John nodded and put on his headset. The calls didn't really get going until an hour or so into the shift, but as soon as you clicked the *Active* button, you were open for business. Luckily, his screen lit up before Ben could make any more small talk.

"Thank you for calling Zinc, this is John, how can I help you?"

Talking on the phone all day might seem like a strange fit for someone unable to hold a conversation, but the disconnect between the physical and verbal shielded him from any discomfort. He enjoyed helping people. He didn't often get the chance outside of a dream. The unseen person on the other end of the line posed no threat to him because of the detachment inherent in the device. There was no risk. Only reward. The difficult part was navigating interpersonal relationships in the office without coming across like a callous jerk. He was happier on calls.

Nine hours later, John walked along the aisles of the pharmacy section of a local grocery store. He scanned the various boxes and bottles for something he had yet to try. Something new. Stronger. A few nights before, he awoke to the sound of his neighbor having a sneezing fit. An interrupted night of sleep was unacceptable. The thought of the lost dreams tormented him. He picked up a name brand box to compare it with that of a knockoff when he heard a voice behind him.

"Is that why you're late to work all the time?"

John turned around and saw Ben holding a plastic grocery basket. He had a two liter bottle of soda with a loaf of bread perched awkwardly on top.

"Not enough sleep?" asked Ben.

John looked between Ben and the pills and attempted a nervous laugh. It sounded like he was clearing his throat.

"Listen, come here." Ben took a couple steps forward until they were close enough to smell each other's breath. "That stuff is no good. My little brother got his wisdom teeth taken out last week but his stomach can't handle the medication they gave him. So, y'know, I was bored and took one and oh man. Knocked me out."

John nodded.

"If you wanna get some good sack time, this is the stuff. Not that," his eyes dropped to the box in John's hand. "Plus, whatever it did to my brother, it did to me too. Stomach issues, if you know what I mean." He waved a hand behind him and arched an eyebrow.

"Oh," said John.

"I've got it out in my car if you want to give it a try. I'm not going to do anything with it. Might as well save a couple bucks on those things, right?"

"It helped you sleep?" asked John.

"Out cold. Not only that, but holy shit did I have some crazy dreams."

John stuck the boxes back on the shelf. "Okay." He followed Ben through the check out and outside to Ben's green pickup truck. John watched as he pulled the handle and dug a little orange bottle out from the storage compartment on the door.

"Here you go." Ben tossed them with an exaggerated arch to John, who surprised himself by catching them.

"Get yourself a good night of sleep. Maybe I'll even see you on time again." Ben laughed as he tossed the plastic grocery bag into his truck and hopped in.

John walked quickly to his car and headed home. Once there, he set the bottle next to the sink in the bathroom and furiously washed his hands. He closed his eyes and breathed in the medicinal smell of the soap. A few moments later, he shook his head and opened his eyes.

He looked at the label as water splashed down the drain. Vicodin. 5/325. He had no idea what that meant. He dried off his hands but left the faucet running, put three pills into his palm, and tossed them into his mouth. He scooped water from the faucet and drank it.

He walked around his apartment in a daze. These pills didn't knock him out like the other pills—they guided him to a more relaxed mindset. He fell asleep two hours later.

The alarm had been ringing for fifteen minutes by the time John grasped for the notebook next to his bed. Once he finished scribbling, he popped out the earplugs and turned off the shrieking alarm. John wrote a few more sentences and finally got up.

Ben was right. The dreams were wild and intricate. He hadn't reached his goal of at least nine hours of sleep, but that didn't seem as important with the way the new pills made him feel. He once read that Carl Jung believed dreams provided messages about lost parts of ourselves that needed to be reintegrated. Well, with these new pills, he felt as if he had found them. He tossed another couple pills in his mouth and noticed he was going to be at least a half hour late for work. He spent the next fifteen minutes making himself a nice breakfast before getting dressed.

The office was alive. Voices commingled to become a wordless hum, chairs squeaked, and the click of the keyboards washed over John as he walked through the push doors of the call center. He was forty-five minutes late but his heart rate remained as slow as if he were waiting out a commercial break.

"Going for a new record today?" asked Ben as John relaxed into his chair. "Almost an hour."

John glanced over and shrugged. The fluorescent lighting above felt softer. He looked down at his hands.

"You okay, John?" He leaned a little closer. "Did those pills help you out at all last night?"

John almost smiled. "Do you know anything about lucid dreaming?"

Ben crossed his arms and regarded John like you might a houseplant that asked you for water.

"There are tricks. Things that are different in dreams that you can learn to recognize. One is that your hands don't look right. They're often bigger and malformed." He held up his hands so Ben could see them.

"You know, I think that is the most words I've heard you say in a row in all of the two years we've been working here."

John looked at the computer screen coming to life in front of him. "And text. Clocks. The part of your brain used in sleeping is different from the part that interprets information, so clocks don't look right. If you get into the habit of checking these things throughout the day, eventually you'll find a time when what you're looking at is off. Then you know you're the other."

"The other?"

"The other you." John leaned forward and logged into the system.

"I think you're the other you right now," Ben said with a laugh. "It's Thursday. Two dollar drinks at Duke's tonight. Do you think the other you will actually come get a drink with us after work?"

John put on his headphones and was immediately greeted with the beep of an incoming call. He turned his head to Ben before clicking the *Connect* button. He shrugged and said, "Why not?"

The bar was a few blocks from the office. Everyone walked down the sidewalk in a group like students on a field trip. The sun had another hour or so before it would set, and John hadn't taken any Vicodin since lunch. The fog was starting to wear thin and he was getting sweaty.

"Can you believe it?" Ben said to another coworker whom John had made the effort not to remember. He slapped John on the shoulder. "The mouse man himself. Finally hanging with the plebeians."

"The what?" asked John. They paused at an intersection to wait for the light to change. "Oh, uh." Ben looked at the man next to him and flashed a smile that was mostly bottom lip. "You know, mice are quiet. It doesn't have anything to do with the rodent part. Just with your tendency not to talk because—"

"Because you choose your words carefully," filled in the other man. John thought maybe he should start remembering him. The light turned green, and the group of eight or nine people started through the crosswalk. Susan led the way.

A few minutes later, John followed the crowd down a flight of stairs off the right side of the sidewalk to the bar entrance below. A bored-looking bouncer sat on a bar stool and neglected to check anybody's IDs as they walked past him. Muted TVs played local news broadcasts. A couple people played pool toward the back of the bar. Neglected dart boards lined the wall near the jukebox and the bar stools along the bar were empty until the crew from John's office filled most of them. The bartender smiled and greeted a few of them by name and soon Ben walked over to John with two glasses of beer.

"Cheers," he said. They clinked glasses. John set his down and walked into the small bathroom where he popped three more pills into his mouth. His hands looked old and wrinkly in the dim bathroom light, but they were unmistakably his own. Three deep breaths and he walked back into the bar.

"Hey John! Here!" Ben held out a tiny, clear glass with what turned out to be whiskey inside. John, not wanting to be rude, accepted the shot and let it burn its way down his throat. He wiped his mouth and tried to smile as his eyes watered. Ben and a couple other people let out a whoop and ordered more beers.

It was unclear exactly how much time had passed by the time John saw Susan speaking with a man at the opposite end of the bar. It was long enough for the pills to join hands with the alcohol and strangle John's mind. Maybe an hour. He was lightheaded and when he tried to check his watch, he was unable to read the numbers. His training kicked in. He straightened out his posture. He looked again to the end of the bar.

Susan wasn't smiling. That was the first thing he noticed. Her eyebrows were low and her jaw was rigid as if frozen mid-bite. The man's back was to John so the only thing he could gather from his body language was that he was big. Finally, she started to walk away when the man grabbed her arm. She paused. John moved.

"Hey!" John said loudly, but not quite a yell. The man didn't turn around. John stepped between Susan and the man and tried to slap his arm off of her. He looked into the man's face and saw a slight smirk grow across his jaw. Just then, the whiskey from before burped its way back into John's throat causing his chest to seize, resembling a cough. A small piece of saliva from the back of his mouth rode the wave of air from his chest and hit the man on the chin. The man's eyes grew wide.

"John, what are you doing?" he heard Susan say behind him. Then everything went white.

He found himself on the floor with everyone around him yelling. Two coworkers had the big man by the arms, walking him away from the bar. John felt a hand on his elbow as Ben helped him.

"What the hell was that?" he said, laughing.

"I need some air," said John as he pushed through the crowd and walked up the stairs to the sidewalk.

The sun was gone but a faint glow still hung in the air. His cheekbone was fiery hot, even through the painkillers and alcohol-soaked fog. He thought about taking a couple more pills but heard a voice behind him before he could reach into his pocket.

"John? What the hell?" It was Susan. She walked up the stairs and stood in front of him as he leaned against the guardrail. He knew it wasn't a dream, but the unreality of the situation mixed with the buzz let him pretend it was.

"Billy got Lyme disease," he said.

She looked behind her as if he was speaking to someone else before turning around. "What?"

"He didn't die or anything. But she clamped down."

"John, what are you talking about?"

"My mother. She blamed herself but it was just nature, y'know?" He let out a deep breath. "He was older than me, so she tried to do better with her youngest. Nothing was going to hurt her baby. Home schooling. Antibacterial soap. You ever meet a dog that was never taken to the dog park?"

Susan looked at him with wide eyes and shrugged.

"They don't know how to play with other dogs. Call it socialization. You learn it young." He sighed again. "I guess I never got to go to the dog park. Stupid Lyme disease."

"John, I think you just need a good night's sleep."

He chuckled. "That's all I ever need. In fact, I thought I already was." He stuck his hands in his pockets and the bottle of pills rattled.

"What's that?" she asked.

"Hmm?" He looked at her briefly before pulling out the little orange bottle. "Did you take those tonight?"

He nodded.

"Jesus John." Her voice softened and the pitch went up a bit. She sniffed even though it wasn't that cold. "Do you need to get some help?"

He pushed himself off the rail and stuck the bottle back into his pocket.

"The only thing I need is a cab home."

"Give me your phone." He did.

She pulled up the app they worked for and clicked the *Home* button for the destination.

Three minutes later, a car pulled up.

"Get some rest," she said. "And maybe throw those things away." He nodded and climbed into the back of the car.

For the first time in years, John didn't reach for the notebook when he woke up. Not because of laziness or the absence of the will to do so, but he had nothing to report. After returning home the previous night, he fumbled his key into the door lock, flipped off his shoes, and fell into bed before he could put in his earplugs or set his alarm. His slumber had been one of restoration, not exploration. He had done enough of that before he went to bed. He peeled himself from his mattress and debated calling in sick. While it was true he didn't feel well, he also didn't want to face his coworkers. Shame flashed through him at every memory from the night before.

But he couldn't find the courage to make the call so he put himself together and called another ride to work. His car sat neglected in the parking garage from the day before.

He paused outside of the push doors of the office and almost turned around, imagining the awkward glances and jokes made at his expense. It had been a while since he made a fool of himself and the humiliation was almost tangible. The calm of the previous day greatly contrasted the rapid heartbeat and shaky hands that welcomed him to his workday. He briefly wished he hadn't left the bottle of pills in his bathroom cabinet at home.

"Well, there he is." Ben came up from behind him and pushed open the door. As if drawn through by Ben's momentum, John followed. "How's the face feeling, Tyson?"

Sore. Red. Puffy. John was so focused on his growing anxiety that he was almost able to ignore his cheekbone. "It's fine."

"Well I gotta say, that was worth the two year wait." Ben sat at his computer and turned it on. John did the same.

"I'm sorry," said John.

Ben turned toward him. "For what? Things happen, man."

John lost himself for the next few hours in his work, refusing to look around the room even between calls. He didn't let himself use the bathroom until lunch break finally came. He waited an extra few minutes for everyone to leave before he first relieved himself, then walked into the break room where a light spattering of applause greeted him. He paused in the doorway.

"Hey alright, man. Take a seat." One of the guys that came to the bar with their group stood up and directed John into a chair.

"Thank you," said a woman from the next table. "It's nice to know we have another one on our side."

John looked at his hands, which were the same size as always. The clock read 12:18. "Here you go, everyone," Susan said as she walked through the door. She held a white cardboard box with a giant cookie in her hands and set it on the table on the opposite side of the room from John. "And," she continued, "let me just say again, finally with you here, thank you to John for helping me with a, well, enthusiastic suitor last night." The group of five other people offered their thanks and congratulations before they started pulling pizza-style slices of the giant cookie. Susan sat next to John, who had yet to grab his lunch from the refrigerator.

"What's going on?" he whispered. "Why are they all cheering me for acting like a big jerk?"

"Well," Susan glanced around and leaned in. "That big guy isn't around, so what's the harm in telling people he was harassing me?"

"Was he?"

"Oh, no. Actually, he was just double-checking what drink he was going to buy me." She smirked but held back a laugh.

"Oh, I'm so sorry."

"Don't be. It's fine. So, maybe you didn't get taken to the dog park, or whatever, when you were younger. I get that. But it's not like they've all been closed down for the last twenty years." She nodded toward the white box. "Why don't you go get some cookie?"

He thought back to three minutes before when everyone was digging in the box with their bare hands. The same hands that had touched the door handle, and the chairs, and God knows what else since the last time they were washed.

"Go on," she said again.

John looked to the box and back at her. She was smiling now. A beautiful, encouraging smile that was so pure and genuine, it felt like it had to be a dream. He thought back to his notebook, and all of the notes of the perfect version of himself. The dream version. Not as an escape, but more an exploration into the possibilities wrapped within him; possibilities that only needed to be recognized to be tapped.

His chair made a light squeaking sound on the linoleum floor as he stood. He walked over to the box, reached in with his normal-sized hand, and pulled out a triangle of the giant chocolate chip cookie. He looked back to the table where Susan watched him, still smiling. He lifted the cookie and took a bite from the end, with no napkin and in front of everybody in the room.

PATIO

I was just sitting on the patio watching the bats fly around when her car pulled up. A faint glow still hung in the sky as the vague illumination of her headlights cut through the thin bamboo wrap circling the patio. I enjoyed another few moments listening to the serene chirps of the blindly circling bats.

The neighbor across the street, that asshole, had been doing some form of construction for the last month, but all I could see were the work trucks that littered the side of our thin road, funneling traffic into the middle. So I didn't pay much attention as the headlights turned off, the engine quieted itself, and the driver's side door opened.

I'd been on edge for months. Nervous. Anxious. But as I sat on the patio with the bats flying above, a train horn in the distance, a lawn mower buzzing somewhere softly, I finally felt at peace.

But then the door closed, I looked up, and she said, "Hello."

The bats continued chirping but I stopped paying attention, leaving me with the fading sunlight and approaching night sky, the bench beneath me, and the overgrown lawn dotted with weeds. There was only me and the voice, and I was taken back to two months prior.

"Goodbye," was the last thing she said.

"Okay," was the last thing I said.

Before that, there were a lot of *buts* and a few *I still love yous* but the order wasn't important. The basic point was that even though we'd spent the last three years seeing each other just about every day, the trend would not continue. It didn't matter that I still loved her and she still loved me.

I would find a roommate. She would do the same. I knew it would be hard to stay in the house; every memory was a scar. The second bedroom that we thought a royal luxury. The broken refrigerator that wouldn't close all the way. But most of all, the patio where I watched the bats before I heard her voice again.

It was a mess at first—a big patch of dirt in front of the house infused with bottle caps, cigarette butts, and for some reason, jagged chunks of broken red bricks. Four flowering perennials concealed more non-biodegradable garbage as they spread their leaves throughout the summer.

We were sick of coming home to a trashy field for a front lawn so we bought some tools.

We moved the plants to the other side of the porch and surrounded them with mulch. The rest was weeded, cleaned, and covered with cement tiles. We screwed together a wooden frame and covered it with a bamboo wrap. We zig-zagged string lights and bolted tiki torches to the posts. We'd pause before walking in the front door after work and I'd put my arm around her, quietly appreciating the structure.

The house was rented but the patio was ours. Planning, execution, expenses—we held the burden for every step and neither of us could have done it alone. This patio was proof that we were not only a team, but a working machine that would fall to pieces without all present parts. This patio was us, and I loved this patio. And then she said "Goodbye," and I said "Okay," and I couldn't look at it for two months.

And then when I finally sat back out there, her voice filtered through the bamboo wrap around the poles.

"Hello," she said.

I couldn't see more than a person-shaped blob through the bamboo, but I didn't need any more than that. The bats chattered above.

"I hope it's okay I came over."

"Yeah." I cleared my throat. "Of course."

"I found a place off of Riverside."

"That's a nice area."

"It's not bad." She stood on the lawn and I still couldn't really see her. I stayed seated on the bench. "Did you find a roommate?"

"No. No, not yet." I felt my lip tremble. I was glad we couldn't see each other. "You know, I haven't signed a lease or anything."

The streetlights clicked on.

"Listen, you can't talk like that." Tears rolled freely down my cheeks. "I just, I don't understand," she said.

I didn't mean to yell, but I did. "Me neither." Then, quieter, "Me neither. It's just, I don't know. It's not right anymore."

"People don't just fall out of love for no reason." She sniffed hard. Her sharp breaths punched through the bamboo.

"Apparently they do."

"But you said you still cared about me."

"I do. I'll always love you but, I don't know. God damn it, that sounds so stupid."

We paused and listened to each other cry. I couldn't hear the bats anymore. With the sun fully set, I couldn't see them either. Then I heard her keys jingle as she pulled them from her purse.

"There's really nothing else to say, is there?"

I wanted to tell her that I was still in love with her, that I wanted her to move back in and we'd get married and laugh every day and make dinner together and build patios for the rest of our lives. But even more, I wanted all of that to be true. So instead, I said nothing.

Then she said, "Goodbye." And I said, "Okay."

THE RAIN

The rain started at about four in the afternoon. It was forecast to pass by to the west, but something shifted. I never understood the jet stream or the different types of clouds. All I knew was that sometimes the sky got dark and it rained.

"It's nothing," said Scott. My husband of five years. He was halfway through his second attempt at college, this time working toward a major in park and recreation management. He hoped to get a job at the nearest state park one day. Working outside had always been a dream of his.

Scott pressed his face against the window over the kitchen sink. He stood on his toes and rested his hands on the countertop. "It should pass quickly," he said.

Meteorology was not included in the coursework for park and recreation management.

But I took his word for granted even though something inside me said he was wrong.

"So are you ready for dinner?" I asked him. Sweet potato enchiladas had been cooling on the stove for about fifteen minutes.

He pushed himself away from the kitchen sink and stood flat on his feet. "I mean I get why social psychology is part of the coursework, like it makes sense, but it's just *so* not what I want to be doing," he said.

His first attempt at college ended about 15 years earlier when he turned 20. Parties had been much more important than his classes at the time.

His shoulder brushed past mine as he walked through the kitchen to what he referred to as his office. In reality, it was an unused second bedroom.

I plated up a couple enchiladas and sat at the table by myself. I tried to introduce a level of normalcy to our marriage—sharing meals, going out together, discussing our days. But as Scott entered his third semester of school, this became much more difficult. I was proud of him for doggedly pursuing his goals, but I didn't like feeling like a roommate.

Was that selfish of me?

The enchiladas were cold, but they were probably still good when Scott came out of his office an hour later and ate some right out of the pan.

"How's it going in there?" I asked him.

He dropped his fork in the sink and set the pan back on the stove. He wiped his mouth with the back of his hand and turned to the window above the kitchen sink.

I walked next to him to glance out at the side yard that runs along the driveway. "This'll fizzle out soon," he said.

"It's starting to pool along the fence."

Scott flipped on the faucet, cupped his hand beneath it, and slurped a mouthful of water. "This rain is starting to make me nervous," I said.

Scott wiped his mouth with the back of his hand. "This water is really cold," he said.

He retreated to his office and I kept my eye on the yard. We'd experienced a few minor floods. The backyard was on a slight incline toward the road, which unfortunately put the house in a vulnerable spot. The first flood filled the crawl space with a couple inches of water. But this is part of marriage and homeownership, we told ourselves. It's not always pretty but there are some things you just have to do. Lugging a dehumidifier into the crawlspace and drying out sludgy puddles among the spiderwebs were part of the job.

Every storm became a cause for concern. A wet crawl space becomes musty and a perfect environment for mold. This can lead to rotting out the foundation of your home and unhealthy air quality.

There wasn't much I could do but look out the window and hope it didn't happen. With Scott in school, we didn't have the money for more proactive remediation techniques under the house. My paycheck from the advertising agency covered our mortgage and bills, but that's about it.

The rain picked up. It sounded like a thousand pebbles bouncing off the roof of our small home. I walked to the bathroom adjacent to Scott's office to get a look at the backyard. A steady waterfall flowed off the roof of the garage toward the back of the property. No gutters, the water splashed onto the dirt below. Growing puddles dotted the backyard.

I knocked on the door to the second bedroom. "Yes?" Scott hated being interrupted.

I cracked the door open and glanced inside. He sat at his desk, laptop open in front of him, with his arms crossed. He didn't turn toward me.

"It's getting bad out there," I said. "I have two more chapters to read."

I nodded and closed the door. Our last anniversary fell on the eve of a big test, so that was just a quick dinner at home. I listened to the rain attacking the roof and leaned against the wall next to the thermostat. It had to have been over a year since we did something together.

I wiped my hands over my eyes and walked back into the living room. Ignore the rain, I told myself. It'll stop when it's ready. It's out of your hands.

So I turned on the TV. Red banners ran along the bottom of the screen, listing counties that needed to watch out for floods. I gave it a moment and saw ours slide by. A newscaster stood in front of a map, pointing at red blobs. I muted the volume but didn't turn off the screen.

An hour passed. The rain continued. I kept my attention on the TV and forced myself to avoid looking out the window. Worrying wasn't going to help.

And that's when I noticed the water starting to leak beneath the side door.

"Scott!" I yelled as I pulled my feet up onto the couch. The water hadn't yet made its way through the dining area. I turned to look at the front door. It was dry, but not for long. I finally allowed myself to turn all the way around and look out the front window.

The drainage ditch had joined with puddles in the road and the front yard, creating a flowing sea. The sea connected our landscaping with the neighbor's across the street.

"Scott!" I yelled again.

The door to the second bedroom flung open and Scott stomped into the living room. "What?"

"Look." I pointed to the leaking door. His shoulders slumped.

"I only have half a chapter left," he said and turned around.

A shiver of electricity ran up my spine. Was this a dream? Did he not see what I saw? I looked between my husband walking back to his office and the water flowing under the door.

Ten minutes later, I stood on the coffee table. Water from the side door made its way into the living room and joined with the water that had started to leak under the front door.

I yelled again. He sloshed his way out a minute later. "You have to stop interrupting me," he said.

"Don't you see what's happening?"

"It's just a little water. It'll be fine."

Was I going crazy? The water was probably three inches deep in the living room. Rain continued to slam into the roof.

"We need to get to higher ground," I said. "It's not stopping. It's *not* going to be fine."

He looked at me funny. I hadn't seen that expression in a long time, probably because I hadn't pushed back at him in a long time.

"Just let me finish—"

"No," I yelled. "We have to go. *Now.*"

He glanced around himself and raised his palms.

"It's a one story house. I don't know where you think we can go."

I pointed to the string hanging from the ceiling in the hallway behind him. "The attic," I said.

He sighed. "I really think you're blowing this out of proportion."

"Our *house* is flooding. Right now. You're standing in water," I said. "You have to take this seriously."

He looked down at his feet, as if he hadn't noticed until just then. He sighed again. "Okay fine, but I'm bringing my notebooks with me."

I climbed off the coffee table and sloshed my way to the small hallway outside the bathroom. I pulled down the folding attic ladder as Scott went back into his office to grab his notebook.

The hot stuffiness that usually made the attic feel like a sauna was a welcome change from the cold water. I didn't care that I climbed right through a spider web. Patches of white dust stuck to my hands and legs as I crawled. I wanted to be out of the water and I wanted Scott to come with me.

Finally, he climbed up.

It was loud. The rain just outside the plywood and shingles sounded like each raindrop was the size of an egg. Gray light fell through the two vents on the roof, with a little more yellow light of the lamps from the living room following us up the attic ladder.

"This is ridiculous," said Scott. He held his notebook in front of him, trying to find enough light to read his notes. His pants were soaked up to his knees. The water was rising faster than I imagined.

"Scott," I said.

He held his notebook in front of him. "Scott," I said again.

He moved the notebook side to side, trying to catch more light. "*Scott,*" I yelled.

He finally turned toward me. "What?"

I could only see half his face. The rain on the roof filled our silence with static. He wouldn't be able to see the tears that had formed in my eyes.

"Don't you see what's happening?" I asked.

He looked at his notebook for a moment and then finally set it down. He leaned forward and tried to look up through the vent. Then he turned around and glanced down the opening into the hallway below. "It's up to the bottom of the picture frame," he said.

Scott turned toward me. The yellow light from the living room lamps lit up his face for only a moment before they abruptly cut out. But in the moment, I saw something I hadn't seen for a long time: recognition.

I climbed over the Christmas decorations and around the neglected luggage to sit next to him and look into the open house below. The water was rising fast.

"What are we going to do?" he asked me.

He put his hand on my shoulder. I couldn't remember the last time he had done that. I had wanted for so long a return to the intimacy we shared in the first few years of our marriage and the four years we dated. But this hand on my shoulder felt foreign. Forced. And uncomfortable. I watched the water continue to rise. I turned to Scott and shrugged off his hand. "It's too late," I told him.

He looked down at the flood as if he could argue with it. His mouth hung open.

My eyes adjusted to the dull gray light. Scott watched me and I must have looked just as pale as he did. There wasn't much light, but I could see the reflection of a tear on his cheek. "I'm sorry I didn't see it earlier," he said.

We didn't say anything else and listened to the rain pelting the roof.

NEAR THE TREE LINE

"Go back inside!" his father shouted. The wind whipped the collar of his coat against his throat. "Now!" David Collins struggled to balance the shotgun in his right hand as the dog pulled on the leash.

Chase didn't move. Even after the divorce, when he withdrew into himself, when his third grade teacher called home about his behavior, when he moved to the new apartment on the other side of town with his mother, he rarely disobeyed his father. He didn't smile much—but neither did he argue. Tonight, however, Chase stood his ground.

They huddled near the tree line at the back of the property, where the orange glow of the light attached to their house became more of a suggestion.

Plenty of things had been left vague in the two years since he first visited his dad after moving with his mother, Hannah. He didn't understand why going to his dad's was called a "visit" when he was going home. Hannah had been calling the apartment their new home, but that didn't make sense. They already had a home. It was right where they left it. There was no room for a new home and nobody visits their actual home; they just go to it.

It was on this first visit that Chase found a dog tied up to the tree in the front yard. "Whose dog is that?" Hannah had asked David.

"It's his," he said, nodding his head toward Chase.

"David, you can't just go and—" Chase's parents walked away, continuing to talk. Chase sat next to the dog he would eventually learn to be a boxer. With its skinny legs and small waist, she didn't seem like much of an athlete, but he didn't name the breed. The dog itself, though, he named after something else he didn't understand.

He liked the word "Brexit" from the first time he heard it while his dad watched the news. It stuck in his head and when David told Chase he could name the dog whatever he wanted, there was no hesitation.

"Do you know what Brexit even is?" asked David with a rare smile on his face. Chase nodded. "It's my dog."

Three years old and housebroken, Chase didn't concern himself with teaching Brexit tricks. Whoever had her before had taken care of the basics. They didn't know how Brexit arrived at the local animal shelter, but David made the impulse decision to bring her home when he heard about the adoption fair. The kennels were becoming overcrowded. And soon, the brown dog with skinny legs and a small waist was introduced to the boy who would spend the next two years essentially attached to her neck.

"Dad, please," said Chase at the light's edge near the tree line.

"She's sick," said David. "You know that. She's not going to get better."

Chase was supposed to be at his new home but he couldn't stay away. They had agreed, his parents, that this was the best course of action and that Chase shouldn't be around. Chase didn't agree with either point.

"This is what the doctor is for," shouted Chase. Tears leaked into his nose which ran into his throat. The words came out soupy. "They can fix her."

"We've talked about this," said David. A quick shimmer of the orange light off his cheek might have been a tear. "It's too expensive for just 'a fairly good chance.' You don't want her to be in pain, do you?"

"No!" But Chase was talking about the pain she would feel that night and not in the coming months. He had noticed the way she wouldn't always get up to greet him. Or the way she would squeak a little when she jumped down from the couch. He loved her—more than anything outside his parents—but he couldn't entertain the thought that the best thing for her was to be gone.

"Chase, honey—" His mother's voice floated on the wind behind him. "Why did you bring him here?" yelled David.

Chase stood between his parents. His mother looked like a dark ghost. The orange light from behind drowned her face in a shadow. She stepped forward and knelt down.

"Chase, things don't always make sense. It seems like they should, but they just don't."

Chase turned around and watched his father lean the shotgun against a tree before leading the dog away from the tree line.

"She's young," said Hannah. "It seems like only old dogs get sick, but that's not true. It doesn't make sense, but that's the way it is." She looked toward David.

"Say goodbye, Chase," he said. "No."

"Chase." His mother left his name to disappear with the orange light in the trees.

He sat in the grass. The dog turned toward him but didn't move. Chase scooted forward and wrapped his arms around her neck. He said goodbye even though he didn't want to. Even though he wasn't sure what death actually meant. Then he stood up and Hannah took him by the hand. His Dad led the dog back toward the shotgun and the tree line. His mother led him back to the house. His home. His first home.

It would be another ten minutes before his father walked back into the house alone. But they didn't hear him close the door because his mother had turned the music up so loud.

SCRATCH OFF

Free french fries.

That's what the sign said, even though the Steak 'n Shake had closed down years before. In fact, almost everything in the city had closed down years before. It started with the aluminum manufacturing plant out by Stones River. That was the first domino. Just under 800 people lost their jobs in one day. None of us could have imagined the ripple effect this would have on the rest of the community. No more lunch breaks from the largest employer in town meant all of the nearby restaurants lost most of their business. Closings began popping up. More people headed out of town to find work. The spread was slow, but constant.

Flash forward a few years and you have Greg Edmonson watching the vinyl banner sign—now only held in three corners, dirtied from years of rain and neglect—wondering what the hell happened to his hometown.

He held tight to the handle on the back of the garbage truck. No matter what happens, he liked to say, there's always going to be garbage. And that equated to job security for him and Don Warren who sat in the driver's seat of the Owsley County Waste Management truck.

Greg watched the abandoned fast food joint disappear behind a hill as the truck eased to the right and pulled into the next neighborhood. They passed Slawson East High School on their left. It had only been six years since he walked these halls himself, but the neighborhood had become almost unrecognizable. Change happens fast. Sometimes, too fast. Street signs were the only landmarks left on a lot of corners.

Finally, the truck slowed and Greg hopped off. He grabbed the first receptacle from the side of the road, flipped the lid, and stopped it in front of the loading arm on the right side of the truck. The control panel sat just to the right where he manipulated the levers as the mechanical arm reached forward, grabbed the canister, flipped it backwards, and set it back down. He then rolled the receptacle back to the end of the driveway and walked to the next.

Just as he had all morning. Just as he had for six years.

"You need a switch?" yelled Don Warren from inside the cab.

Greg shook his head. "Nah, I'm good."

Truth was, Greg loved his job. It wasn't the most glamorous gig but he got to work outside in the morning. He had a steady paycheck. And after all, there's always going to be garbage.

They continued along their route for another hour or so until a glass bottle of Miller High Life exploded across the pavement when it reluctantly rolled out of the receptacle just a little too late.

People rarely packaged their trash the way they were supposed to. Recycling would come on Thursday. All the person had to do was put the bottle in a different container, but there were always mistakes. A shattered bottle was hardly worth recognizing. Greg only glanced down momentarily, but it was enough to notice the small, green index card lying in the broken glass.

"Hold up," said Greg after rolling the canister back to the curb.

He bent down and saw it wasn't an index card at all. Soaked in stale beer and covered in tiny shards of glass, he wondered if the scratch-off sections of the ticket would scratch off at all.

"Come on man, let's go," said Don from the inside of the truck.

"Just a minute." Greg picked up the soggy lottery ticket and walked it up the passenger side door. "You got a penny?"

Don leaned over and dug through the fast food wrappers and empty disposable coffee cups that littered the seat.

"Here you go." He tossed a nickel through the window which somehow Greg caught. "What'ch you got?"

"I got our retirement plan right here." Greg leaned the soggy ticket against the door and dragged the coin across the silvery sections. A line of numbers along the left side of the ticket acted as the goal. All of his numbers lined the right side. "Just gotta match one and we get a hundred thousand."

"Finally," said Don.

It wasn't uncommon to find the occasional treasure. Mostly, that meant appliances that weren't actually broken, stereo speakers, or maybe a book. It wasn't quite dumpster diving if it never went into a dumpster. The fact that so many people were moving out of town meant that they'd rather get rid of a lot their stuff than haul it across county lines.

An untouched scratch-off was rare, but not out of the realm of possibility.

Greg uncovered all the numbers along the left side and went to work on his own numbers. All he needed was one match. Maybe he could bring home a nice dinner to Kayla.

There were two matches.

"We got two chances here to change our lives," Greg said to Don. "God willing."

He knew you were paying for the hope and not the prize, so he liked to drag it out and keep that hope alive just a bit longer.

He scratched off the prize for the first matching number. Twenty dollars. "Heyo, ten a piece," said Greg.

Don smiled and shook his head. "Not bad not bad."

He scratched off the second prize and felt his fingers go numb. He looked between his number and the winning numbers but had trouble focusing his eyes. He stared at the prize for another moment.

"Holy shit," he said quietly.

"Hey man I'll take the ten. That ain't bad for a free ticket."

"No," said Greg.

"Now now, you know the rules. Whatever we find we split. That's the way it's been for years."

"No, not that." Greg held the ticket up to the open window. Don leaned forward and squinted his eyes.

"You know I can't read that," said Don.

Greg checked one more time before looking to Don and saying: "We won."

"How much?"

The feeling returned to his arms and he finally allowed himself to smile. "All of it."

They let the ticket dry in the sun on the dashboard beneath the windshield. They knew they couldn't just go down to the corner store to cash in $100,000 so they'd figure out what to do once they were done with their route. Turns out they needed to head to a state lottery office and wait for a check to come in the mail. It took a week to process and could only be sent to one address, so they chose Greg's. He'd found the ticket, after all.

Driving trash routes that week had been almost unbearable. The excitement between them made the process of grabbing, emptying, and replacing cans of garbage insignificant. But until the day that check came in the mail, it wasn't real.

Kayla called him the moment she found it in their mailbox.

"I can't believe what I'm looking at," she said to him through the phone. Greg stood on a street corner over by the empty shell of a Piggly Wiggly. "All those zeros. I never seen anything like it."

Don came over that night and picked up a check for his half.

"You wait a day or two to cash that until this clears, alright?" said Greg as he handed it off.

Don smiled and wrapped his arms around Greg's shoulders. It was the first time they had embraced in the six years they worked for Waste Management. They had only been in the same truck for three, but their friendship went back to high school.

Kayla and Greg sat at the kitchen table with the check with all the zeros in the middle.

Greg took a deep breath and looked at the ceiling for a moment. Everything was going to change. It might not have been enough to retire on, but $50,000 would go a long way.

"This is it," said Kayla. Greg nodded.

She stood up and wiped her hands across her eyes.

"I can't believe we're finally going to get out," she said. "Wait." He sat forward. "What?"

"This is enough! We don't have to sell the house before leaving. We can just go. Sell it when we sell it."

"Hold on. Who said we're going?"

Kayla stopped pacing and turned to her husband. Three years of marriage hadn't been easy. Inheriting the house from his parents sure saved them a lot of time and money, but that didn't stop the city from crumbling around them. She hadn't been able to hold a steady job since graduating high school. Not that that was her fault; everything kept closing down. Serving, hostessing, she even worked at an oil change garage for half a summer. She took any job that came her way but they never stuck around for too long.

"When did I ever say I wanted to leave?" He stood up. "Just think of it. We can finally fix the roof. Put in a deck in the back. Get a real AC system and get rid of these stupid window units." He smiled and reached for Kayla's hands. "We can make this place everything we wanted."

Kayla pulled away and walked across the linoleum floor of the kitchen.

"You said you wanted to live somewhere new. See things you' never seen before and all that."

"That's just something you say. Like wanting to go skydiving or backpack through Europe."

"No it's not. Not when we're the last people on Earth in this town." Greg closed his eyes and held them.

"Kayla, please. This is a good thing."

"Not if you plan on using it to stay here. I *hate* it here."

"This is our home."

"This is your *parent's* home."

"They gave it to me because they knew I'd take care of it. It's my responsibility. And now we can do that!"

"They gave it to you because they knew you needed it. Matt should have gotten it, being the oldest and all."

"So what? So what if I like it here?"

"You don't like it here either," she said. "You're just too chickenshit to try anything else. I don't give a damn about the AC or the roof or whatever." She took a step forward and softened her voice. "Greg, please. We have to get out of here."

He looked at his wife but could only see the kitchen behind her. The countertops his mom used to top with flour when she made chocolate chip cookies. The sink where he and his brother used to fight over who would wash and who would dry the pans. The back door his dad used to prop open when the room got too warm while mom yelled at him to stop letting in the bugs. He couldn't see the future she had planned for them but he could easily see the past.

"We're not going anywhere," he said.

She turned around and walked out the back door.

Greg and Don didn't talk much about the lottery ticket over the next week. Instead, they kept whatever decisions they were making to themselves and carried along the day's route like normal. It wasn't until the start of the next week that Don told Greg he only had one week left.

"What?" asked Greg. They stood outside the truck in the parking lot of the Waste Management facility. At three in the afternoon, the sun still hung high in the sky.

"Going back to school. I've been looking into it for a while but wasn't sure if I could make it work. Now I can."

"That fast?" Greg leaned a shoulder against the truck and took a deep breath.

"50 grand ain't gonna change your life, but it can help you do it yourself," said Don.

"Wow," said Greg. He couldn't believe he had to fight back tears. "I'm gonna miss you, man."

He drove home in a daze.

Comparison is a huge part of life no matter how hard you try to avoid it. You frame your experiences—your accomplishments—against those around you. And as long as you have someone comparable in your life, whatever you're experiencing doesn't seem so bad. Don had become Greg's comparison—justifying his stay in town, his job, basically his way of life.

Without Don, how would he convince himself he was doing fine?

He parked in his driveway underneath the basketball hoop that hadn't been used since he was in 9th grade. Things had been tense around the house. The local news picked up the big win and ran it as the feel-good story at the end of the broadcast. The reaction from the community was mostly congratulatory, with a few exceptions.

The roof of the house had a slight wobble to it that had become less and less slight over the years. It wasn't leaking—that he knew of—but he didn't feel comfortable moving into another winter with it. That was at least ten grand right there. He knew the plumbing underneath the house needed some work, too. But that's the advantage of it being under the house; it's easy to ignore a degrading water heater until it completely stops working.

Walking through the door was the same as it had been for the last week. A terse hello from Kayla. No hug. No kiss. She hadn't given up on the idea that they'd use the money to leave. Greg hadn't given her any indication this was a possibility.

How could winning all this money be a bad thing?

Kayla walked outside, most likely to tend to her garden. He enjoyed the fact they could eat something that came directly from the dirt of their property. It might not be much—a zucchini here and there, lettuce, some peppers—but it was something. They didn't have any kids. They didn't have any pets. They only had each other and the items they could produce together. Garden vegetables were one of these things. $50,000 had become another.

Greg watched her through the kitchen window. She stuck her fingers into the soil to check the moisture. A few dead leaves had to be picked off. And it looked like those damn beetles were back.

The phone in his pocket vibrated. Phone calls had been rare up until the news story. He sighed and pulled it from his pocket.

"Hello?"

"Can you hear me from your pile of gold coins?" asked Matt Edmonson, Greg's brother. "Ha, yeah. Yeah just fine."

"You know I was scrolling through my Facebook feed and I come across this news story somebody posted and it's a picture of my brother saying he pulled in a hundred thousand."

"Well, yeah they never really mention that I had to split it with my coworker."

"You did?"

"Yeah. But listen, half of a hundred thousand still ain't bad."

Matt visited once every year or two. He moved out and went to college ten years before and never looked back. He found a job managing the finances of an insurance outlet and upgraded apartments every couple years. He always said he hated moving but not as much as being bored. A new neighborhood seemed to keep him occupied.

"Yeah I guess not," said Matt. "So what's the big plan? Buy your big brother something real nice?"

Greg laughed. "I'd light it on fire in the backyard long before that."

"Hey jeez."

"No, I'm not sure yet. There's so much to do around here. Place is falling apart." There was a brief pause. Greg watched Kayla adjust the cucumber trellis.

"So you're going to put it into the house?"

Greg nodded even though it was a phone call. "I'm thinking so." Another pause.

"Greg, what do you really have going on around there?" He leaned against the counter top and closed his eyes.

"Did you talk to Kayla or something?"

"Why did she ask the same thing?" asked Matt. "No, I didn't. But I'm not a dummy.

Anybody could tell she wants to get out of that house."

"But this is *our* house."

"No, it's Mom and Dad's house."

"That they left to me. I don't know why nobody gets that. Mom and Dad left this house to me when they passed. It was important to them. They knew that I'd take care of it. This is the only house they ever owned. They worked hard for it. They wanted it to stay with the family so they left it to me because they knew you'd just sell it."

"Did they say any of that?" asked Matt.

Greg rubbed his closed eyes with the thumb and forefinger of his free hand.

"Did they actually come out and say they wanted the house to stay in the family? Or is that just what you thought?"

"I know that's what they wanted."

"No you don't. They gave that house to you because they knew you needed it. That you weren't going to go anywhere. The truth is, I don't want anything from you. But if Kayla has been asking you to use the money to get the hell out of that stupid town—I mean look around you! What's left?"

Greg looked around the kitchen. The dining table sat exactly where it had when they were kids. All the family dinners at that table. Dad sitting in his chair balancing the checkbook.

Bracing himself against the side of it when he got the phone call about their car accident. This house was more than just a house. It was more than walls, windows, and a floor. Why couldn't anybody else see that?

Matt sighed. "Just think about it, okay?"

Kayla walked in through the back door and glanced at Greg. He held up a finger to tell her to hold on.

"Sure. Listen, I gotta go." They said goodbye and hung up.

"Do you wanna go out for dinner tonight?" asked Greg. "We never really celebrated the win."

There was a wall between them but it would come down eventually. Just not yet. "To where?" she said and walked out of the room.

It was still early in the day—another hour or so and the sun would start to slip toward the horizon. There was nothing to do around the house so Greg walked outside. He looked at his car in the driveway. The wavy roof. The lawn he kept short so the weeds could be mistaken for grass.

He turned down the sidewalk and started walking. The house next to them had been empty for a while. The Schultz's moved out last year and sold the house to a developer that must have run out of money. He was sure it would be knocked down eventually and rebuilt like they had been doing all over town. The running theory was that eventually people would realize how inexpensive these new houses were and start buying them up. The city wouldn't stay dead forever. But the rebuild would take some time and investment. These big development firms were able to take the hit normal people couldn't absorb.

Greg followed the same path he'd taken every day to elementary school. He took a right at the end of the block, walked another two blocks, took another right, and stepped off the sidewalk onto the wood chips of the playground. He thought about sitting on one of the swings when a car pulled around the corner and floored it. Greg turned toward the noise in time to see an arm come out of the back window and launch something white at him. An egg exploded on the sidewalk ten feet to his right.

The car reached the end of the block and turned.

Greg sat on a swing. It didn't feel that long ago that he was riding around town being a teenage asshole. The boredom of being in your hometown seemed to be a universally-shared experience. Everyone says they want to move out, go to New York, see the big wide world. But how many people actually do that? Everyone says they want to play in the NFL too, but you rarely meet a professional linebacker.

Being the middle of summer, the schoolyard was empty. The only kids running through the playground were the ghosts of his memory. Childhood was a time for hope. For potential.

High school graduation was when you needed to give up on being an astronaut, drive down to the Waste Management facility, and accept the realities of your life.

He thought about his brother. And Kayla.

Were they still under the illusion that people could actually be whatever they wanted? Or did they temper their expectations just a little less than he had?

The afternoon heat wasn't so bad when the breeze ruffled his hair as he pumped his legs. Kayla didn't have an attachment to the house.

Her roots weren't as deep as his.

Was he being selfish? Isn't marriage supposed to be a give and take?

He swung higher and higher. Eventually he could see to the parking lot of the school at the peak of his swing. A man wheeled a trash can to the dumpster. The janitor didn't get the summer off. There's always someone at the school even if only a handful of kids showed up to make use of the summer rec program.

Is this what he imagined when he ran through this field as a kid?

A light *tink* rang out as the chain gripped in his right hand snapped. He tumbled sideways through the air and landed hard in the woodchips. But nothing hurt. Nothing throbbed. The woodchips weren't exactly soft, but they cushioned his fall despite the impressive slam.

Fifty thousand dollars. Greg spent his adult life holding onto the familiar because the fantastic was only a dream. But now that dream had come true. What did that say for the familiar?

What's the point of staying the same when everything around you is constantly changing?

He stood up, brushed himself off, retraced his steps down the street, took a left, walked two blocks, and took another left. Kayla sat on the porch when he again walked past the Schultz's abandoned house.

"Hey," she said. "Are those woodchips hanging off your shirt?"

Greg sat down next to her and looked at the neighborhood. His neighborhood. But maybe not hers.

"We're not going to get much for the house," he said. "But it'll be better than nothing."

I COLLECT TEETH

A lot of people think teeth are made of bone. They're not. Your humerus can heal itself after a break, but a chipped tooth stays chipped forever. Teeth can't regenerate. If anything, your teeth are an absolute liability. Ignore them and they'll kill you. Gum disease introduces bacteria to your bloodstream and before you know it, you're scheduling an angioplasty.

This is why I collect teeth. Not to ward off heart disease (that's what flossing is for), but as a reminder that even the most mundane aspects of our daily lives contribute to the end.

I found a bag of my baby teeth in my mother's sock drawer when I was in high school. The clear, plastic sandwich baggie was surprisingly heavy as I passed it from one hand to the other like a slinky. The roots were so long, it made the part that chewed the food seem inconsequential.

Mom never mentioned the missing bag of teeth after I transferred it to my own room. It felt appropriate, stealing the bag like that. These teeth were originally stolen from me. I left them out for a magical fairy, not my sneaky mother.

I'd get back at her eventually, in a way. It turns out cremation isn't actually a bonfire that torches the body to ashes. It's more like an oven turned to 1,800 degrees. Have you ever cut onions too small and found them as crispy little flakes after baking them too long? It's like that. And maybe the crematorium was in a rush that day, but I was able to find many mostly-full teeth in the bag of ashes I was given at Mom's funeral.

The collection grew.

People sell all sorts of strange things on the internet; mummified raccoon penises, stillborn shark fetuses, and baby teeth.

The working days of these teeth are long gone, but I catalog them just the same. Whether they were found in my mother's sock drawer, a bag of ashes, or purchased online—they deserve a level of respect.

If you go to a well-organized workshop, you're likely to see a catalog of various screws. Different sizes, different types, all of them separated and labeled in a storage and filing system so the woodworker knows exactly where to find the materials they need.

I kept a series of drawers with little note cards on the ends in the spare bedroom of my house. It was ostensibly a reading room, with a little desk and filing system that you might glance right past if you were touring the house. In fact, it took a few visits from Franklin before he noticed.

"What is that? Dewey Decimal cards?" he asked. We had been together for maybe two months. It was the longest relationship I had in years.

I simply shook my head and directed him back to the kitchen where I was finishing up a batch of lemon garlic orzo with roasted vegetables.

It wasn't a secret—the teeth. The subject was simply very hard to explain without looking like a crazy person. But realistically, any type of collection is a little crazy. Nobody needs 50 pairs of sneakers they'll never wear. Nobody needs action figures locked forever inside their original packaging. Every collection was essentially a well-organized hoard, albeit of a specific type.

I'd show Franklin eventually. I'd try to explain why teeth were so beautiful—the understated necessity of care, the unseen support system, the brute utility of them. But of course he didn't understand. He just saw a collection of bones—even though they're not bones—and remained hypervigilant until he walked out of the house for the last time.

My mother would have understood. There had to be a reason she held onto my teeth all those years until I reclaimed them. And as I sat down at the desk after Franklin walked out, I knew he wouldn't be back.

You don't choose your interests. They emerge from the ether and you either run from them or embrace them. Not everything is the way it seems. Teeth and icebergs share an unseen majority. Sure, we all know it's there, but it takes an extra moment of thought to actually consider what is hidden beneath the surface.

Teeth are part of who I am and how I interact with the world around me. If we just met, the first thing I would do would be to analyze your mouth. I wouldn't have fantasies about pulling your teeth out or anything like that. But I'd take the time to consider what you have chosen to show me, what is hiding behind that façade, and what version of neglect is going to end up closing out your final chapter.

DROWNING
WITHOUT SINKING

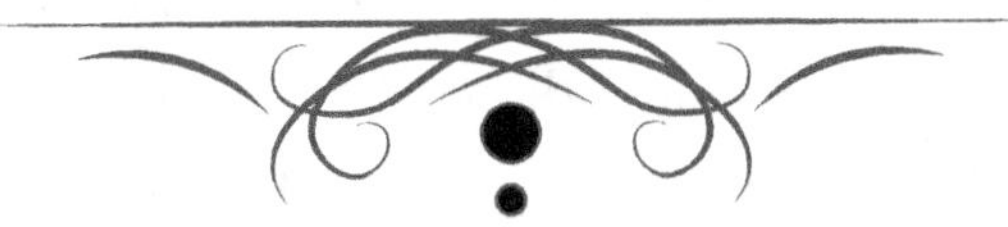

The first time I drowned was at night. Whitney and I had only been dating for a month and I wanted to show her that I could be spontaneous so we climbed the fence at the public pool. The air was cool but the excitement and nervousness kept our blood warm and rushing through our veins. Her silhouette was outlined by the full moon as she stood on the diving board. I treaded water below her even though I hadn't taken the time to teach myself how to swim all that well.

The pavement along the side of the pool scraped my back as she dragged me out of the water, but I didn't feel it. The bright, white light from the moon illuminated her beautiful, yellow hair as she pushed the water from my lungs. It wasn't a conscious thought, and I didn't realize it until much later, but that was the moment I fell in love with her.

"Thank you," I said.

The second time I drowned was at a Memorial Day barbecue with my extended family.

Whitney had moved out, but we hadn't signed the divorce papers. In fact, we could still be considered newlyweds, but the pregnancy was further along than our marriage. Filling my lungs with water turned out to be a great way to avoid the awkward questions and monotonous silence from family members that never really knew me all that well in the first place.

Afterwards, when they dragged me across the sand and pounded on my chest until the water erupted from my mouth and nose, I felt refreshed. My eyes drank in the blue sky and yellow sun with a fresh thirst. Colors were deeper. Scents stronger. I dusted myself off, shook my wet hair, and smiled up at my Uncle Bob.

"Thank you," I said.

The last time I drowned was in the winter. We were ice skating, me and Andy. I taught him how to slide to a stop, throwing shaved ice in front of himself like a fan of frozen water. He was halfway through his fourth year of elementary school and his best friend had just moved away. I tried to explain that this was, in fact, a great lesson but he was still too close to it. He needed some time.

The lake was large so the wind had no impediment and picked up a respectable speed, but we didn't need gloves or hats. Maybe I should have expected the ice to crack, but it still took me by surprise.

The water bit into me and I couldn't find the breath to yell out. The lake consumed me. Sunlight filtered through the ice and left the lake in a silent haze. After a moment, I didn't feel the water. I couldn't hear Andy yelling above me. I waited until it was time to become the lake. And when the joining happened, I wasn't afraid.

Andy would need some time to understand, but again, I knew it was an important lesson. My only hope was that maybe, one day, he himself could drown and understand the beauty of the undeniable connectivity of life.

THE TRUTH

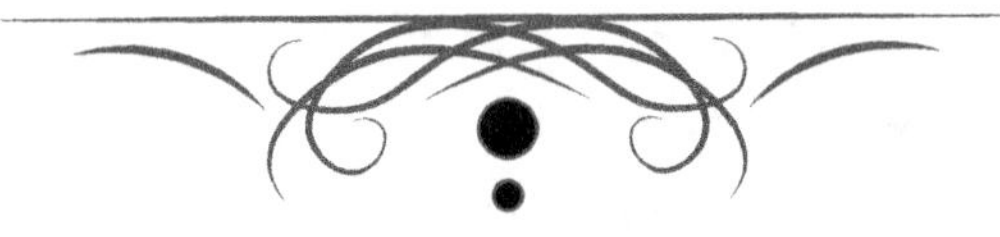

In my younger years, I valued honesty above all else. The objective truth. Even if it made things worse. But how does that saying go? Be careful what you wish for because you just might get it?

I'm older now. Not to the point of worrying about the balance of my 401k, but old enough to question the beliefs that built up my abstract sense of being. The version of myself that only resides in my head. If I were religious, maybe I'd be questioning that. But I'm not. The closest thing I have is my long held insistence on truth. On logic. On reality.

When you get right down to it, the truth is something most people shy away from—and for good reason. The truth is that the world is not a nice place. Cute animals get eaten by ugly ones. Innocent children get mangled in car wrecks. And sometimes, your boyfriend says something like: "I hit my last girlfriend."

"I just wanted you to know," is what he said next.

Everyone thinks they're smart. Even stupid people. Maybe *especially* stupid people. Even the people with a self-deprecating sense of humor, deep down, think they're special. It would be impossible to muster up the energy to pay bills, go to work, and pursue romantic relationships if a person thought they were just some piece of shit taking up space. Even if that were the truth.

"Why are you telling me this?" I sat at the kitchen table. The marinara sauce was starting to harden on the plate in front of me. A warm scent of tomatoes and garlic surrounded us.

He was such a hickory tree—solid, steady, historically handsome—when he first approached me at the grocery store.

"I think bananas are bullshit," he said to me. We weren't even in the produce section. He told me later he just thought it was a funny way to start a conversation. He was right.

He didn't have a problem with tiny lies back then, maybe three months ago. Why the insistence on absolute truth now?

"I feel so guilty." He hadn't finished his pasta and I couldn't take my eyes off of the remnants on the plate in front of him. The parmesan cheese had hardened. The steam was long gone.

I didn't love him. Not yet, anyway. I think I've always valued my time more than myself, so proximity went a long way when it came to love for me. I've only had one relationship last more than a year but we said that word to each other. Love. I believed it was true at the time. Looking back, I wonder if I thought I felt that way simply because I gave him so much of my time. You should only give away that which is most important to you to someone you love.

If other people don't view their relationships as transactions, they're lying to themselves. "Why?" I asked.

He set his fork on the torn paper towel to the left of his plate. It was quiet. The record on the turntable needed to be flipped. He shrugged and looked up at me. "Because she didn't deserve it."

"No, why are you telling me this?"

He didn't keep a journal. He didn't feel the need to chime in whenever he had an opinion. Give him a few drinks and he'd get a little gushy, but I never saw him cry. All together, he was a great companion—there for you when you needed him and mostly unobtrusive. He had a temper but it was based in frustration. If there was any anger, it was directed inward.

"I thought you should know," he said.

The truth doesn't exist on its own—it needs someone to vouch for it. But without that support, it's just another sentence dancing its way to oblivion.

You can tease it out, if you have a suspicion. The truth. You can ask questions, wear someone down, but the truth doesn't just appear. It doesn't have its own momentum.

An image of him raising his hand to some faceless woman flashed through my mind. I didn't like it so I shook my head. I stared at the pasta but couldn't get that moment out of my head.

"I don't want to hear this," I said and stood up. "I don't want there to be any secrets."

I wanted to tell him that I don't care about secrets as long as I never find out. It's the only way to erase the terrible past. It's a simple measure of self-preservation that for some reason is looked down upon. But why? A confession only serves to bring someone into your circle of shit. I couldn't tell him that, though.

"So what am I supposed to do with this? Be afraid?"

"No!" He stood up a little too quickly and his chair squeaked on the linoleum floor. I was glad it didn't fall over.

A well-placed lie can change your whole life. A poorly-placed truth can ruin it.

I looked across the table, over the plates and glasses and hardened cheese, and studied him. This man that seemed like he could absorb bullets. His eyebrows pushed together in the middle in a way I'd never seen before, as if he had just asked me something and was waiting on the response. But he hadn't asked a question, all he had done was completely change the air between us with a hope we could still breathe the same.

The image of him raising his hand in anger flashed through my mind again. My younger self would have told him that I needed some time to work this out. That I needed to figure out how this made me feel. I would think that was the strong thing to do. But I wasn't that girl anymore. I didn't need to kneel down to the altar of the truth if it meant chasing away the only decent man I'd felt at ease with for years.

The truth isn't static. It can evolve over time, especially when it comes to interpretations and emotions.

I put my hands on the back of the wooden chair in front of me and looked down at the plates on the table between us.

"I'm glad you told me," I lied.

LUCKY

My order always waited for me on the counter at the liquor store by the time I reached the front of the line.

71-8-9-49-81-7

The same six numbers every week. It never occurred to me they would actually match the ones on the little ping pong balls on the television towards the end of the news, until it happened.

I won 34 million dollars.

My chest felt like it disappeared.

Things had been difficult ever since Jacob's mom died a year before. He's only seven, but it doesn't take long before the other kids sense weakness. And nothing hurt me more than thinking about Jacob being pushed around at school just because his mother didn't brake hard enough.

I sat on the couch with the ticket between my hands. Jacob was already in bed. Thoughts exploded through my head before I could catch them. I would've thought I'd go running to my son's bedroom. That I'd wake him up with shouts and hugs. But that's not what happened. My heart was racing all right, but it wasn't from excitement. Fear flooded into every breath. The odds of winning were somewhere around one in two-hundred million. And I had hit that sliver of a chance.

I thought about how many times I'd driven down any particular road, and even more, how many times the road had been driven down in general. It's an unfathomable number that only grows. And how many times had I driven past an accident? Once a week? Twice a week?

The odds of those unfortunate drivers not making it home are incredibly small, just like winning the lottery. So why did Rebecca find herself trapped behind the driver-side door after a pickup truck slammed headfirst into it? If you were looking strictly at the odds, you'd have to say my wife was lucky.

Good luck and back luck are the exact same thing.

Falling into a sinkhole, being struck by a meteor, cars running up onto sidewalks—all of it not only seemed possible to me, but probable. I just won the lottery. What's stopping me from hitting the 1 to 280,000 odds of being struck by lightning?

I turned out the lights and TV, walked into my bedroom, and put the ticket into my desk drawer. The bed sheets were cool but it wouldn't be long before my body heat warmed them up. I turned out the light.

I turned off the alarm on my phone a minute before it was set to go off at 6:30. Sleep hadn't been an option. Every passing car or unidentifiable shout could have been a masked disaster. My legs felt like they weighed 50 pounds each as I pushed myself out of bed.

I knocked on Jacob's door as I walked past and went into the kitchen to make some eggs. I flipped on the gas stove and stared at the flames. I saw explosions and burned flesh. Fire alarms rang in my ears over the screams of people trapped behind locked doors. I turned off the heat and got out a couple of bowls for cereal.

"Good morning, Dad." Jacob climbed into a chair at the kitchen table. I asked him what he wanted to drink, which was obviously going to be orange juice. I alternated between scooping the cold cereal into my mouth and gathering his things with my free hand. Scoop. Grab his backpack. Scoop. Stuff his books and folders inside.

"C'mon buddy. Go get dressed," I said as I set my bowl into the sink. He climbed out of the chair without a word and went to his bedroom.

Twenty minutes later, we made it out the door and into the car. I pulled out of the driveway and gasped when I saw the traffic at the end of the street. Cars zoomed by in both directions. Fear wrapped itself around my chest tighter than the seat belt. I slowly turned right.

"Do you know what *luck* is?" I asked.

Jacob turned his head and shrugged. "Isn't it like something that helps us?"

"Yeah, yeah that's the idea."

He was quiet for a moment. "Why?"

"We, uh, we got some good luck last night, bud."

"We did?"

"Yeah, we did." It had been a while since I could give him some good news. It helped me believe it was good, too, even though it didn't feel that way.

"What happened?"

I eased on the brakes as we approached a red light. He stared at me for a moment and I let that hope and expectation hang between us. He wasn't smiling, but he was close to it. I hadn't seen a smile on the way to school since Rebecca's accident. He told me how much he hated it, but I figured every kid hates school. I guess I didn't want to believe the bullying was as bad as it actually was—and then I saw the bruises. He begged me once not to make him go, but there didn't seem to be any other option.

"Did you remember your math book?" Of course he did. I put it in his backpack myself.

He nodded and I eased my way through the intersection, glancing quickly in each direction to make sure there weren't any street sweepers with faulty brakes or stoned teenagers ignoring their red light.

I turned on the radio and occasionally ventured a glance over to see him tapping along to the upbeat rhythm. We arrived at the school before the song ended.

"Alright bud, you be good."

"Okay."

I gave his knee a quick squeeze before he hopped out of the car. I waited until he walked through the doors of the school and glanced in the rearview mirror. Jacob will be safe in there. Won't he? Yes, of course he will. I drove home with both hands on the wheel and my eyes firmly focused on the road.

Driving Jacob to school had been terrifying but necessary. He has to go to school. Only unfit parents take their kids out of school. In fact, that had been a bit of a fixation since Rebecca died. She was always the one to go to the school meetings since I was usually at work. I didn't feel comfortable there after she passed, so I avoided it. The way they looked at me—I could tell they were all just waiting to find a reason to call social services.

I wasted my day checking mortality rates of car accidents and trying to distract myself with daytime TV. Before I knew it, it was three o'clock and time to head back to the school.

After a quick breathing exercise, I grabbed my keys, walked to the car, and started driving.

I was a mile away from the school, waiting at a red light with the radio off. The light turned green and I pulled forward. A car entered the intersection to my left. His tires squealed and in the moment before I locked up my brakes, the image of Rebecca's crushed car flashed past my eyes. I screamed until my car came to a stop then looked to my left where I saw a middle finger hanging out of the window of the car.

I pulled over and turned off the engine. My hands shook and little white dots filled my vision. I unclipped my seatbelt and abandoned the car as the other lunatics zoomed past me. I ran down the sidewalk. I didn't want to be late and risk Jacob thinking I had forgotten about him, or worse, an abduction.

It was only a mile, but I'm no runner. I found Jacob standing next to the flag pole when, wheezing and sweating, I finally arrived. Mr. Parson, his homeroom teacher, stood next to him.

"Dad?"

"Jacob. Hey. Don't, don't be afraid." I put my hands on my knees and spat between my shoes. "I'm here. You're safe." I put my arm around his shoulder and scanned the yard around us. In my mind, there was a line of unmarked, windowless vans in front of the school just waiting for the next parentless child to wander onto the sidewalk. "Let's go home, bud."

"Jim. Are you okay?" asked Mr. Parson.

"Yeah, yeah I'm fine."

He looked at me like I had an extra eye in my forehead. We had to get home, behind a locked door, as soon as possible.

"Where's your car?"

I turned Jacob away from his teacher and looked Parson in the face. "It's somewhere else." I locked my eyes on his. My jaw rigid.

The teacher put his hands up and took a step backwards. "Okay, okay."

"Where's the car, Dad?" asked Jacob as we walked down the sidewalk.

"It's sick. Just like when you had that sore throat last month," I told him as I scanned the street for errant drivers and rabid animals. I hated lying to my son but I didn't want to tell him that cars only invite accidents. I didn't want to remind him what happened to his mother.

Twenty minutes later, we walked into our apartment and I locked the door behind us. I told Jacob the car would probably be gone for a while. I thought that if I was forced to leave my apartment, I could just buy a tank. As long as we were home, we were okay. Excluding natural disasters. And stray bullets. And poisonous spiders.

Two weeks passed. My employers did me the favor of firing me after the first week of not showing up. The school seemed to be reaching a tipping point as well, after two weeks of Jacob showing up late to school, if I was able to get him there at all. It shouldn't have been a surprise when there was a knock at my door just after we sat down to dinner.

I looked through the peephole for about five seconds before I said, "Who is it?"

"Damon Ball. Social Services. Could you open the door, Mr. Bennett?"

I hesitated.

"Identification?" I said. I watched as he dug in his pocket and pulled out what looked to be a card. It was impossible to read it through the peephole. I unlatched the lock and cracked the door open.

"Let me see that," I said. He held the laminate closer to my face.

"Mr. Bennett, I'm just following up on some questions we've been receiving about the welfare of your child."

"Questions? By who?"

"It seems Jacob has been missing a lot of school lately."

"We've been busy."

"And his teachers were troubled by your appearance. I'm just here to make sure their worries are unfounded so we can put all of this behind us. May I come in?"

I looked behind me at Jacob sitting at the table. "I can't let you in here."

"Sir, I have to say that your behavior is aligning pretty well with their concerns. If you allow me to disprove them, we can forget about all of this. But if you insist on blocking my inquiry, I'll be forced to come back with the police."

"Well then go get your backup," I said as I started closing the door.

He stuck his foot in the crack, leaving the door open a few inches. "Listen, Jim is it?" he asked, a little quieter than before. "I gotta tell you, this looks bad. I know your wife is gone and I don't want you to lose your son, too. He hasn't been coming to school and your behavior's...well, weird. You can't go on like this if you want to keep Jacob around. We only want what's best for him, but at the same time, we want what's best for you. I don't want this to get nasty, but if you force me, I'll have no choice. Now please, let's just put this to rest."

I held his stare for a moment. Anybody can make a laminate. I turned to look at Jacob, sitting at the table staring back at us, and imagined if he wasn't there. An empty table. An empty life.

Back to Damon Ball. He didn't look like a bad guy. Which right was most right?

"Wait here," I said. "But let me close the door, please." He withdrew his foot and I flicked the lock. "Be right back," I said into the peephole.

I glanced at Jacob as I walked past and managed a smile while I held up a finger to him as if saying, *Just a second.* I walked into my bedroom and pulled the lottery ticket from the drawer.

Jacob picked at something and I could hear the fork twinkling against the plate. Other than that, complete silence. I focused on the ticket. The talisman. I stared at it. I felt the thin, waxy paper between my fingers and rubbed my thumb over the printed numbers. And then I saw it.

71-8-9-49-81-7

It was a mirror of itself. A palindrome. A perfectly balanced number that fell back into itself the same way it started. How had I not noticed this before? I'd been playing the same numbers for years but I never thought about what they meant. I opted for the computer-generated ticket the first week and then simply stuck with the numbers. It was accidental, but a sense of balance was created all the same.

A prickle went up my arm. The winning ticket wasn't an example of an exorbitant amount of luck which could apply to anything at all, good or bad—it was a rebalancing of my equation. I had a large chunk of my life amputated when I lost my wife. Maybe this was the universe's way of attempting to fill that hole. Nothing could replace Rebecca, but removing any type of financial worry would go a long way toward reclaiming happiness. My son needed to be there with me to do that.

I walked to the front door and swung it open. Damon Ball was on the phone but he quickly slid it into his pocket.

"You want an explanation of why my son hasn't been to school? Here you go." I showed him the ticket.

"I don't understand."

"Have you seen the news stories about the winner of the lottery? How he hasn't come forward?"

He nodded.

"You're looking at him."

He didn't say anything for a moment. He stared into my eyes, waiting.

"We're moving. That's why I've been keeping him home. We're getting ready to go and I wanted to ease him into it. That's also why I haven't gone to work. I haven't claimed it yet because I don't want to make a big deal before I'm sure Jacob is ready." I put the ticket into my pocket. They weren't exactly lies. It sounded like a pretty good plan.

He stayed quiet for another moment before nodding. "Okay, Mr. Bennett. I'm not going to close this quite yet but once I see you claim that ticket, I'll have no choice." He glanced inside the apartment at Jacob, sitting happily at the table. "You two have a good night." He started walking away. "And congratulations," he said.

I closed the door, ignoring the lock, and sat at the kitchen table.

"Who was that?" asked Jacob.

"Nobody. Don't worry about it." I pushed my plate to the side. The food had gone cold a while before. "Do you remember that luck I told you about on the way to school? When we still had the car?"

He shook his head.

"That's okay," I said. "Well, here's the deal. You don't have to go back to school." Jacob knocked over his glass of water. He didn't move and neither did I.

"I mean, you'll still have to go to school, but not this one. A different one." The water cascaded off the side of the table and began slapping the floor. "We're moving."

His eyes grew moist and a hint of a curl etched around the corners of his mouth. We listened to the water drip onto the tile below the table for a moment. "To where?" he asked.

I stood up and walked around the table, avoiding the puddle next to Jacob's chair. I kissed him on top of his head and put my hand on his shoulder. "Wherever we want," I said and set the 34 million dollar ticket on the table in front of him.

FEATHERS

At first, Mom was Mom. Red hair, long fingers, quick smile. We'd dance together in the kitchen. She'd take me to soccer practice. Every night before bed she'd tell me, "I love you." And when I started asking about her cough, she added, "I'm okay."

One day, Mom became a caterpillar. She was still Mom, but she moved slower. She danced slower. She said less, but she still said, "I love you. I'm okay."

Then Mom wrapped herself up in bed which became a cocoon. Over time, the blankets fused to her body. The cotton became a membrane; a protective barrier from the threats her inefficiencies failed to repel.

She stayed like this for a while. She even moved from her cocoon at home to another building with a lot of cocoons. The whole time, she told me, "I love you. I'm okay."

Everyone was surprised when, one day, Mom changed again. Doctors and nurses came running into the room. Dad stood next to her bed, but I stayed back and let the adults try to exercise control over the uncontrollable. I knew my Mom was okay. She would always be okay because I love her, and she loves me.

I think they expected her to turn into a butterfly. Maybe that was why they rushed around so much. But she didn't change into a butterfly. Instead of layered scales of colorful exoskeleton, feathers emerged. They were so white they almost seemed to glow. They covered her from the crown of her head to her now claw-like feet.

She stretched her wings and they filled the length of the room. Everyone stood back as Mom crawled from the cocoon and shook her feathers. She stood on the bed with the torn cocoon covering the mattress beneath her feet. The doctors and nurses took a step back with wide eyes and fingers spread. My father reached a shaking hand toward her which she took and glanced at him but only for a moment. Then, she looked at me, smiled, nodded, and flapped her massive wings once.

She broke through the window and joined a host of birds as they flew through the sky. I had to look away as they flew directly toward the sun which seemed to devour them as they disappeared within its glare. Despite the shining sun, despite the ease of flight for my Mom and the others, rain poured down from unseen clouds and gave the feeling of two different days existing within one.

Everyone in the room was silent, but I think I was the only one who heard her say, "I love you. I'm okay."

I wasn't sad as I watched her disappear into the sunshine. Birds are always around, and I knew she would be, too. I can feel her watching me from the fence post or power line. The morning song of unseen birds is drenched in her voice.

We still dance together. She still watches my soccer games. And I still know that I'll be okay because she's okay, and she loves me.

FIREWORKS

Olivia couldn't imagine what her life would be like without the bakery. Late mornings had been her evenings for a long time. Pastries and doughnuts turned into pumpkins around noon, as she liked to say. Cakes lived into the night but she had Cheri to help with those.

She stood in the parking lot of the bakery but didn't open the door to her 2020 Camaro. It took her a while to get over the embarrassment of driving such a flashy car, but you don't get to choose the prizes. Reality shows have sponsors. Even the baking competitions. She leaned against the driver's side door and looked back at the sky blue building. It had been a coffee shop for a year or so. Then it was a vacant eyesore. Then it became the black hole that sucked up her prize winnings until opening day two years ago.

She took a deep breath of the crisp, spring air and felt the phone vibrating in her pocket. "Hello?" she said as she closed her eyes. You can say you get used to waking up at 2 a.m. but it still wears on you.

"Olivia."

"Samantha." She hated how her sister-in-law started conversations like she was activating a virtual assistant.

"We need to talk."

"Good thing we're on the phone, then." Olivia stuck her free hand into her pocket and palmed her keys.

There was a quick burst of static through the earpiece as Samantha huffed out a quick breath. "You need to mind your business."

Olivia looked back to the sky blue building. "I am. Why? Is something wrong?"

"Not the bakery. I mean—you know what I mean."

"No, not really actually. I'm sorry."

"My marriage," Samantha said. "I know you've been talking to your brother." Olivia nodded. "Yup. Just about every day for the last thirty years."

"*Enough.*"

Olivia waited for Samantha to continue but the silence was scarier than what she wasn't saying. Olivia scrambled through her memory to find a slight. An errant comment. Something that might set her sister-in-law off. It was no secret that they would never go on vacation together, sharing secrets and giggling over dinner. But Olivia thought she did a pretty good job of keeping everything civil. Samantha didn't make much of an effort, but no one really expected her to. A dinner without Samantha calling someone a dipshit was a success. Olivia began to worry something had slipped through her filter, but couldn't even remember the last time they were together longer than a few short sentences.

"Lucas' decisions are his own," Samantha said. "And I won't have you spilling poison into his ear."

"Poison?"

"Olivia, are you really that stupid?"

Olivia squeezed her eyelids shut and faced the warm sun. Another static sigh.

"A divorce isn't going to happen. Okay? No matter what you *think* you know about our relationship, or what you want Lucas to think about it."

Divorce? Had Samantha read her mind or something? "Listen, Samantha, I don't know what you think—"

"Save it. Just save your bullshit," Samantha said. "I know you and Lucas are real close or whatever but I'm his wife. Okay? He *chose* to marry me. No one chooses who their sibling is.

That's just dumb luck. Or a curse. So stay away."

"Stay away?" Olivia had the keys gripped in her fist but couldn't feel them. "What do you mean?"

"So you really are that stupid." She hung up.

Olivia continued holding the phone against her ear for a moment, repeating the conversation in her head. When did she mention divorce? Her face grew hot. Her hands shook.

She unlocked her car and climbed inside. She remembered a conversation in Lucas' Malibu a few days ago. But it was just the two of them. There's no way Lucas would mention it to Samantha. Would he?

Lucas sat at a red light in the very same Chevrolet Malibu his sister was thinking about. It wasn't a bad car. Not as flashy as his sister's, for sure, but he didn't want anything that would make people turn their heads as he drove past. That just seemed annoying. In fact, he was shocked when she told him she was going to be on TV. Not that she wasn't good enough. She won the whole damn thing, after all. But she was just too measured, too kind for a reality show. Even a cooking competition.

The light turned green and he started forward, but a black truck apparently decided it was still his turn. Lucas slammed on his brakes and missed a breath. He sat until he got a few good ones into his lungs before the car behind him gave a honk. Lucas glanced at the little dash cam attached to his rearview mirror. It might be nice for insurance, but it won't mean anything if I don't have a head anymore, he thought.

He drove so defensively he annoyed himself for the rest of the drive home. He hoped the Andersons liked the little two bed one bath ranch-style home they had walked through this morning. It wasn't much, but it had character. Their price range wasn't going to let them go much bigger, anyway.

He pulled into the driveway and parked next to his wife's hatchback. He didn't expect her to be home, but her schedule changed every day. Maybe he'd have to wait until after dinner to head into his little makeshift studio in the garage. The potter's wheel was just plain fun.

"Hey honey," he said when he walked in the kitchen.

She stood in front of the refrigerator with her arms crossed. "How's it going?" he asked.

"I just got off the phone with your sister," she said. That was a surprise. "Oh yeah?"

"Did you know she thinks we should get a divorce?"

He set the manila folder with a printed copy of the house listing, a few scribbled notes, and the business card of the homeowner's realtor on the table.

"She what?"

"You don't want to get divorced, do you?" Samantha turned toward him but kept her arms crossed. He used to tease her that her arms would fall asleep, keeping them crossed like that all the time. Everyone said it was a defensive stance, but she wrapped herself up whether she was laughing, crying, and everything in-between. In fact, she had her arms crossed the first time they spoke outside of Mickey's Tavern. It was the first thing he noticed about her. The first thing he liked.

"Of course not," he said.

She walked toward him and stopped a few steps short.

"I don't want to get divorced," she said quietly.

"Neither do I." He made up the last few steps and wrapped his arms around her. Her crossed arms jabbed into his ribs.

"I know we've had our problems," she said. "But we can't have this kind of talk. These ideas. They fester and grow."

"I agree."

She finally released her grip on herself and wrapped her arms around Lucas. "So we agree?"

He nodded again.

A few breaths passed and she let go. Something didn't feel right. "Wait, about what?" he asked.

"That we shouldn't see your sister anymore," Samantha dropped her arms and walked into the living room.

Lucas opened his mouth but the breath again disappeared.

The sun had been staying up noticeably later, but it would be another couple months until it reached its peak. No light fell through the windows of the garage. Well, no natural light at least. The harsh, white light of the fluorescent bulbs hanging from the rafter above cast a slight shadow over the potter's wheel. Lucas preferred working while it was still light out, but you had to take what you could get.

He couldn't get the clay centered. Nothing would work if it wasn't centered. He leaned his weight onto his left hand on top of the hunk of clay, but the right hand couldn't steady it. His foot pushed too hard. Then too soft. The required fluid motion wasn't there. He sat up and shook the water from his hands. He glanced over at the shelf of drying pots, many more than there used to be at any given time, and sighed.

There was no way to expect what Samantha had told him. At the same time, it wasn't a shock. Olivia wasn't exactly shy about her feelings about Samantha.

Earlier that week, they were on their way to the farmer's market. It was one of the things they did together. There were many.

Farmer's markets in the spring didn't have much more than eggs. Lettuce, beets, and asparagus didn't trip their trigger this week. So after wandering around and enjoying the almost-comfortable weather (still a little too crisp) they hopped into the Malibu. "See, we could've taken your hot rod," said Lucas.

"Can't risk having dirty root vegetables rolling around on the floor. You understand." Olivia set a carton of eggs between her feet.

"Oh perfectly." Lucas wiggled his way out of the parking spot and hopped into what passed for traffic in their small town.

"Not much there today, was there?" she said.

He shook his head. "Even the stupid crafts were particularly stupid today. Did you see the ceramics guy?"

"So you're some big ceramics expert because you got a wheel off eBay and use it once a month?"

"Actually, I use it quite a bit these days." His voice came out a little quieter. A little softer. He eased to a stop at a red light.

Olivia turned in her seat. "Oh yeah?"

"Yeah. It's nice to get out there."

Olivia nodded and waited a couple breaths. "Things getting bad again?" she asked.

Lucas looked out the window. There was a tree across the street and that's about it. "I mean, distracting yourself with ceramics is good, but it's just a distraction Lucas."

"I know," he said.

She watched him but didn't speak for a moment. The light turned green and the car lurched forward. "I know you love her.

Okay? I know that. But I've been holding my tongue on this for a long time."

He glanced over at Olivia.

She adjusted herself in her seat. "Okay, how long has it been since you've had a good day with her?"

"Just last—"

"A *whole* day. Waking up to going to bed."

"Well, I mean—" His voice trailed off. He flicked the turn signal.

"That's what I'm saying. You wouldn't be in the damn garage all the time if you enjoyed being inside the house. People change, Lucas. And that's okay. But sometimes they change, well, apart from each other."

"Olivia, I'm not going to leave my wife."

Now it was her turn to look out the window. They stayed that way until he dropped her off ten minutes later.

Lucas knew his sister and his wife didn't get along. But they didn't have to. All they needed to do was be civil with each other. And for the most part, they did that. He thought they did that as a favor to him, but that had obviously stopped.

He stood up from the potter's wheel and stretched his elbows behind him, pushing out his chest. The garage had become the most comfortable place in the house. The fact that it wasn't actually in the house wasn't lost on him.

And now that Olivia had taken her gripe directly to the source, the whole thing had imploded. Why the hell would Olivia do that? He stretched his elbows behind him again and released a deep breath, but the tightness in his chest wasn't going anywhere.

Lucas knew he couldn't leave his wife, no matter how bad it got. She'd kill him.

The next morning, Olivia sat on a stool pulled up to the prep table. Her laptop glowed brightly with a spreadsheet of vendors, invoices, and dates splattered across it. She had trouble focusing on the numbers. A short redhead that walked faster than some people ran whipped a whisk in a bowl behind her.

"You ever think about denying someone a cake?" asked Cheri.

Olivia turned around. "Excuse me?"

"Yeah, you know, just tell someone *No*."

"Why would I do that? You know how business works, right?"

"Do you?" asked Cheri.

Olivia turned back to her laptop. She sighed and closed it.

"I don't know anymore." She stood up and left the computer on top of the stainless steel tabletop. She couldn't begin to guess how much dough she'd smashed across that space. Enough to feed a small school for a year, at least.

"Hey." The whisk stopped its rhythmic tap against the side of the bowl. "What's up with you?"

"Nothing, Cheri. Don't worry about it."

"Your name's on the sign. Not mine. Even though my macarons were a hell of a lot better than yours—"

"It's been *years*, Cheri."

"—and somehow that British dickhead chose your plate instead of mine. So you know what? I do worry about it when our fearless leader turns into a mouse. I don't want to get a real job."

Olivia leaned against the wall and almost smiled. "Well, you know how important my family is to me."

"I know how important your *brother* is to you. I still say you two should just date and get it over with."

"That joke is never going to be funny."

"What joke?"

Olivia sighed. "Samantha thinks I want Lucas to get a divorce."

Cheri crossed her arms. "Well you do, don't you?"

Olivia nodded. "Yeah. Yeah I do. She's just so *mean*. He deserves to be happy instead of just thinking he's happy."

"Right, but is that your job to do something about it?"

"Cheri, when we were kids, and someone was picking on me? He sure did something about it."

"So why did you tell her that?"

"Tell her what?"

"That you think they should get a divorce."

Olivia pushed herself off the wall. "I didn't say that."

"So why does she think you did?"

It was Olivia's turn to cross her arms. "You know what? That's a good question."

It's late. Well, it's late for Olivia. Pushing 8 o'clock is basically midnight to her. So when her phone rang it almost made her jump off the couch. She steadied herself and reached for it on the coffee table. It was Lucas.

She stood up.

"I don't know if you're supposed to be calling me," she said.

"Well, that's why I'm calling you. What the hell happened?"

"I don't know! She called me yesterday and just, like, well she was just her super pleasant self."

"Cool it. Okay? It's all this shit that got this whole thing started in the first place. You know how awkward this is for me? I'm right in the middle of something I had nothing to do with."

"I'm sorry."

A pause. Olivia walked into her kitchen. Reality television fans would be extremely disappointed how little this kitchen was used.

"I'm guessing she doesn't know we're talking."

Lucas sighed. "No. of course not."

"Jesus. So how long is this going to last?"

"Well—" The unfinished sentence hung in the air. "How long?" Olivia repeated.

"Do you remember the Bouchard sisters? In like fourth grade or whatever?"

"Yeah."

"So you remember when they held you down in the snow and gave you a face wash?"

Olivia nodded. The handfuls of snow dragging across her frozen skin felt like tiny razors even though they didn't make a scratch. "It was terrible."

"Okay, so then you remember how I took off the front wheels of their bikes and buried them in the snow by the dumpsters?"

Olivia smiled, but that didn't stop the tears forming in her eyes.

"They had to walk to school for a week until Billy What's-his-name dug them out? They were pissed. Like level ten pissed. Do you remember what happened after that?"

Olivia didn't say anything.

"Nothing. Janie wanted to rip my head off but I talked her down. We were playing on the playground by the end of the week. But Samantha holds a grudge longer than a fourth grader missing half her bike. I stood up for you then because it didn't matter to me whether I talked to the Bouchard sisters ever again. But this is my wife, Olivia. And no matter what you think of our marriage, I have to live with her. I don't have a choice any more than Janie and Mel had to be sisters."

"That's not true," Olivia said quietly.

"Yes it is. Now, I don't know why you would tell Samantha why we should get a divorce—"

"What?"

"—but that doesn't even matter anymore. Samantha doesn't change her mind when it's made up."

"Wait, Lucas. Wait. What are you saying?"

"We shouldn't be talking."

Silence.

More silence.

"Ever again?" she asked. More silence.

"I love you," he said.

Neither of them spoke for a moment. He waited for a response, and she held the sob bubble building in her throat.

Finally the line clicked dead.

Three months passed. It's late morning and the summer sun was already uncomfortably warm. Olivia had finished her morning duties and was aimlessly clicking through old invoices on her laptop. Her phone sat lifeless in her pocket. Nothing but work calls and messages since early spring.

"Big day coming up," said Cheri. Her apron showed streaks of white down the front but it was unclear if it was actually from today or not.

Olivia turned away from the screen. "What?"

Cheri blew a puff of air out of the corner of her mouth. "It's the end of June."

"I know."

"And what's at the start of July?"

Olivia nodded. She knew. "I know."

"I know you know. Isn't the Fourth of July like your favorite day ever? Christmas and Halloween and your birthday all rolled into one?"

Olivia shrugged, but Cheri was right. Ever since she was a kid, the Fourth of July was this weird day of the year when she got to be an adult. There was no way her parents would give her a bomb in the middle of September. But it was totally fine at the start of July. The whole neighborhood was outside either grilling food or eating grilled food, and Olivia and Lucas were basically left to their own devices. The best part was that their mother hated fireworks. Couldn't stand the noise. So ever since Olivia was eight and Lucas was ten, they went to the fireworks on their own. There were so many kids around that nobody even noticed two young children without supervision. Of course, Lucas' supervision was as tight as a school counselor's. He made sure they found their spot, that his sister didn't wander out of his sight, and they made it home as soon as the show ended. Thinking back, Olivia was surprised their overly-protective parents left them alone like this, but you can't argue with history. Once something happens, it happens. And now Olivia was learning that all over again.

"Oh come on, you can't seriously just skip the whole thing just because you are in a fight with your brother," said Cheri.

"It's not a fight." It's a disownment, she thought.

"Why don't you just text him? He can always pretend it's from someone else if what's-her-name is there."

"I don't want to make things any harder for him."

"Alright, listen." Cheri walked up to Olivia but didn't sit down. "I've been watching you mope around all summer. I know this sucks for you, but more importantly, it sucks for me.

You're not even enjoying the work anymore." Olivia nodded.

"What was it you said on the finale of that show? Your bullshit little speech?"

"I don't know. That was years—"

"Oh yes you do. You know, I still think that's why they picked you over me. It certainly wasn't that crème brûlée." She paused. "Magic. You said baking was like science mixed with cooking mixed with magic. And of course that *captured the hearts* of the nation and boom they give you the golden ladle or whatever."

Olivia smiled. It came across cheesy, but she meant every word of that speech.

"You can still have fun even if you're not talking to your brother. He wasn't the reason you loved the Fourth of July. He was just one aspect of it."

"I don't know."

Cheri groaned, grabbed Olivia by the hands, and pulled her up.

"You're acting like you got dumped by your brother and I don't have all the time it takes to explain why that's disturbing and weird. Things blow over. Okay? And this is going to blow over, too."

Olivia sighed. "You don't know this woman."

Two in the morning on the Fourth of July is the same as 2 a.m. on any other day of the year. It's dark. It's quiet. And the only people awake are bakers and drunks. Olivia went through the motions but wasn't really paying attention to her work. She couldn't stop thinking about how it would feel sitting at home and hearing the deadened thuds of fireworks through the walls of her house.

Cheri walked in at seven.

"Happy Fourth!" she said with a smile. Olivia offered a quick wave. "Oh come on. You can't be a sad sack piece of shit all day." Cheri walked over to the iPad connected to the Bluetooth speakers, poked at the screen a few times, and turned around as the opening ring and snare snaps of *Born in the USA* jumped from the speakers.

Olivia, arms out and palms down, tried to mime to Cheri to turn it down. Cheri only danced over to her.

"We're going to the fireworks tonight."

"Cheri, please, I gotta come in here tomorrow morning anyways—"

"I don't care."

"I really don't—"

"I'll be at your house at seven. Get drunk first if you need to, but I don't care—we're going." She danced her way back toward the speakers, singing far too loud for seven in the morning.

Olivia spent the rest of her afternoon alternating between finding excuses to bail and talking herself into it. Cheri was right, after all. Her enjoyment of fireworks and all things related to the Fourth of July didn't come from her brother, but they were inextricably related to him.

Like herself. Would she still enjoy the warm glow of fireworks cascading from the dark sky with Cheri? Why wouldn't she? And at the same time, how could she?

Her phone rang late in the afternoon and her mood sank. It had to be Lucas. Nobody called anymore. Cheri would definitely text. She ran from her bedroom into the living room where her phone sat on the coffee table. Disappointment ran through her like the flu before she picked it up. It was Cheri.

"I'll be there in an hour. Are you drunk?"

"No."

"Fix that. I'll be there in an hour."

"You already said that."

"See you in an hour."

Olivia set the phone back on the coffee table and collapsed into the couch. She felt every minute of waking up at 2 a.m. Her legs ached. Her fingertips throbbed. And more than anything, she didn't want to walk into the parking lot of the abandoned Kmart to set up folding chairs near the elm tree in the back corner. People didn't want to be near trees when they were looking at the sky. But what most people didn't understand is that you don't look straight up. Lucas told her this when she was eight.

Finally, an hour passed and she heard a car honk outside. Olivia grabbed her chair and a bottle of water on her way out the door. She could hear the chime and beat of *Born in the USA* as soon as she stepped outside.

"Still?" she asked as she opened the passenger side door of Cheri's old Jeep.

"Born down in a dead man's town! The first kick-a-kookas bena-bena ground!"

"You don't really know the lyrics, do you?"

Cheri smiled and nodded her head too hard with the beat.

"Boooorn in the USA!"

Cheri pulled out of the driveway and Olivia turned down the music.

"You know that song's not really all that positive, right?" said Olivia.

"Born in the USA. What's more positive than that?"

"Maybe you should actually look up the lyrics sometime."

"Who needs lyrics why you have USA right in the title? It was made for the Fourth. Cheri turned the music back up and left the song on repeat until she parked the car twenty minutes later.

"You know," said Cheri as they climbed out of the car, "you might've been right about that song."

"I know."

The neighborhood streets were lined with cars. Locals drank beer in their front yards and waved at families walking past. Cheri and Olivia had to walk in the street to avoid a little girl drawing a massive mural on the sidewalk in front of her house. Neither of them could tell what the object was, though. Groups of people surrounded them, laughing, yelling, and chasing each other. Olivia smiled as she watched, but her expression didn't match her mood. Everything was tainted. Slightly skewed. It was like sitting down to eat your favorite meal to find it was seasoned wrong. Everything looked familiar and enjoyable, but it was not.

"See?" said Cheri. "Shining sun, people laughing—it's still the Fourth."

"Yeah," said Olivia.

They walked over a small patch of grass to the parking lot. Muscle memory led Olivia to the right. There were a couple chunks of concrete that were buckled from when they removed part of the loading dock years before. It's amazing the old Kmart was still empty, but really the only thing they could've put in there was another doomed department store. It was better to leave it a skeleton. The parking lot was already half-full of families and groups, but the area beneath the elm tree was empty. It was always empty. They set up their chairs and stretched their legs in front of them.

"How have I never noticed this spot is wide open?"

Olivia shrugged. "No one does."

Over the next half hour, they sat in silence and waited for the sun to disappear behind the tree line to their left. Cheri stood up as it got close.

"I'm gonna pee before the war breaks out." She walked toward the porta potties near what used to be the loading dock.

Olivia slouched down and leaned her head against the back of the chair. Her folded hands rested on her belly and she tried to pay attention to the soft rise and fall of her breath. The chair next to her grunted as Cheri sat back down. She waited for a slap on her shoulder to wake her up. Instead, a familiar voice spoke softly.

"How many of these fireworks do you think it'd take to get Illinois to surrender?"

She opened her eyes and looked to her left where Lucas sat in Cheri's chair.

The show always opened with an attention-grabber. Lucas called it the appetizer. A quick burst of six or seven medium-sized blasts filled the sky that had yet to go totally dark.

"Lucas!" She stood up and wrapped her arms around his neck. He tried to pat her on the back but, being seated, couldn't get the right angle.

"Where is she? Is she here?" asked Olivia.

"Who me?" Cheri walked up from behind Olivia. "Oh hey, Lucas."

He waved.

"Sure, yeah, go ahead and use my chair. I hate sitting."

"Oh sorry," he said as he started to stand up.

"No, no, no." Cheri waved her hands in front of her. "Take it. If you can get Olivia here to stop being such a sad sack, it's worth it. I'll go sit on the curb over there. You two talk." Cheri patted Olivia on the shoulder and walked away.

Olivia sat back down but scooted her chair closer to Lucas'. It's hard to have a conversation when explosions punctuate your sentences. "So where is she?"

"Samantha's at home."

"Does she know you're here?"

"We're in a bit of a fight."

"How did you know I'd be here?" she asked.

Lucas smiled. "Where else would you be?"

A giant red candle streaked across the sky, tinting their faces and everything around them. "It was the dash cam," he said.

"What was?"

"I couldn't stop thinking about why she would call you. Just out of the blue like that. I realized you had no reason to just be like, *Hey Samantha, Lucas should divorce you.* People don't do stuff like that."

A loud pop and then everything went green. A group of high schoolers to their right shouted sarcastic *oohs* and *ahhs.*

Lucas continued: "So I had to figure it out. I went through every scenario for months and finally I got into an accident. Nothing big, someone cut in front of me and boom. But they tried to say it was my fault, and the trusty dash cam proved them wrong."

Another white blast.

"But you know what I realized when I pulled up the video? That thing has sound. I could hear myself saying *Oh shit!* And I could hear the crunch of the accident."

"The dash cam," said Olivia.

"I asked Samantha if she pulled up the video of when you and I went to the farmer's market. She tried to tell me she had almost gotten in an accident and wanted to see the video and accidentally heard our conversation, but that was bullshit."

Olivia sat forward as three fireworks momentarily erased most of the shadows in the parking lot.

"She was spying on me. Lord knows how many times she listened to me sing along with the radio before she heard something juicy. We kinda had it out after that."

"Wow," said Olivia. "I can't trust her."

"My ass hurts." Cheri stood behind them. "It's great you came to see your sister and all but you could've brought a chair."

"Oh, sorry." Lucas stood up, walked around to Olivia's side, and sat on the ground with his arms wrapped around his knees.

"Damn right," said Cheri as she sat back down.

They sat in silence as the fireworks painted the sky in beautiful blossoms of color—each bright flash punctuated with dark pauses. During one of these pauses, Olivia leaned over and asked: "What's going to happen next?"

The sky lit up with a bright white willow.

Olivia and Lucas looked at each, nodded, and stood up as smiles grew across their faces. "What's going on?" asked Cheri?

"Grand finale," said Lucas.

And just as they had every year for the last twenty-two years, Olivia and Lucas took breaths as big as they could. The first blast of the grand finale rang out and both of them screamed as loud and as long as they could in an effort to outlast the barrage of explosions.

Neither of them had ever come close. The flashes of sound and color continued as their screams devolved into wheezing whimpers and finally, laughs.

HOPI

The screaming started about a month before the sky burst into flames. Her voice came out full, fevered, shrieking in response to seemingly nothing. Betsy and Robert first marveled at the sound of it. Even as a baby, wrapped in a blanket alone in Woodland Park, the officers heard no protest or complaint as they brought her to their station. And then into the group home. And finally into the arms of a retired school teacher and her equally retired husband.

Hopi. It was embroidered on the back of the blanket. A singular loving act presumably from her birth mother. Those four letters were the only clue to her past. They figured she was around one year old when she was found. They also figured her mother had abandoned her, although any imagined scenario was equally true. Betsy told herself Hopi's mother had been in trouble. That no one would leave such a perfect example of innocence to the whims of the outdoors given any other choice. Whatever her past, her present was healthy and hopeful. An even-tempered baby turned into a laconic toddler turned into a mute child. Betsy thought she noticed a smirk once as the child slept. She assumed she was mistaken. By the time Hopi found her voice, she'd made it five years without so much as a grunt.

It wasn't a nightmare. Or an injury. Hopi stood near the sliding glass door that led to the backyard. Betsy was putting the breakfast dishes into the dishwasher. Robert was reading at the table. Over the next month, they would try to figure out what started the screaming, but you can't find a reason for nothing.

Hopi's young body had seemingly saved the last five years' worth of speaking energy for this singular performance. Inhalations were the only break. One sustained note grew more distorted as the day went on. Once the sun had set, Hopi's body became wracked with exhaustion. Betsy was able to convince her to chew a few crackers and drink half a cup of water before she fell asleep for the night. At dawn, it started all over.

Betsy and Robert called every doctor in town. They were told a variation of the same thing every time: Speak calmly to her, she'll tire herself out.

The doctors were wrong.

This went on for weeks. Betsy and Robert began wearing earplugs around the house and communicating through hand signals. The neighbors complained, but what could be done?

And then, day 29 of continuous screaming, the sunshine filtering through the windows changed color. Yellow became a dancing orange. Betsy and Robert were too busy trying to make sense of a sky filled with flames instead of clouds, and didn't notice the return of silence.

Mouths agape, they stared into the sky. No sun. No wind. Just fire spreading to the horizon. They were close enough to see individual spires of flames licking the atmosphere, but far enough that the heat was only a suggestion. For now. Betsy turned from the window and pulled the plugs from her ears.

"Robert?"

She looked at her husband of 42 years and slapped him on the shoulder. He turned around, reached into his ears, and dug out the yellow foam.

"Robert, where's Hopi?"

They looked around the house, made sinister by dancing shadows in the orange light. No sign of her.

They rushed to their cars and drove around the neighborhood. Betsy called Hopi's name from the driver's side window as Robert stared into the sky. The road didn't require much attention as all the other cars had either pulled over or stopped where they were. Occupants craned their heads out of their windows and stared above. People on the sidewalk did the same. The constant movement above was hypnotic.

"Hopi!" she continued to call.

They zigzagged through the neighborhood until they passed Woodland Park. The playground was empty. The baseball field and basketball courts were abandoned. One person-shaped object appeared toward the back of the park near the tree line. It was the exact spot a couple officers, responding to a distressed 911 call, found a small girl with no history wrapped in a blanket.

Betsy stopped the car and got out. "Hopi?" she said tentatively as she approached. The child was lying on the ground with her hands behind her head. She looked into the sky as if it weren't crawling with flames, but filled with fluffy clouds waiting to be interpreted as animal shapes. Hopi briefly shifted her gaze to Betsy, motioned her head to the ground next to her, and returned her attention to the sky.

Betsy looked back to the car where Robert continued craning his head out of the window and looking up.

"Hopi? What's going on?"

Hopi again motioned to the ground next to her.

Betsy sighed and did as she was told. It took a couple moments to get her elderly frame onto the grass, but soon she felt the grass tickling the back of her neck. She glanced to her right at Hopi. Betsy felt the child's hand wrap around her own. Earlier that month she heard the child's voice for the first time. And now, underneath a wall of flames, the heat drawing beads of sweat from her forehead, she saw another first from the child that has shared her home for the last four years.

Hopi was smiling.

Betsy found herself doing the same.

RACHEL + JEREMY

Familiarity sits on the opposite end of the spectrum from discomfort. From the time Jeremy was small, new foods new friends new rooms had always increased the rhythm in his chest and added an inconsiderate amount of sweat. He thought "being in a rut" got a bad rap. Hiking trails were essentially ruts that everyone agrees are the best route through the forest. If life is a forest, wouldn't you want to be in a rut?

His route down the sidewalk of 2nd Street might as well have been a worn path. Lunch break from Coleman & Schuster Financial Advisors afforded him more than enough time to grab a soup/sandwich combo from the diner down the road and revel in the familiarity of the neighborhood. Hardware store. Bank. Office building. It was stock footage rolled out at the same time over the course of the workweek and it felt to him like a room painted a nice manganese blue. Comforting. Almost meditative. With all this familiarity, one would think Jeremy would have remembered the tree that had overgrown its three-by-three allotment in the sidewalk, roots shrugging the surrounding cement blocks creating small lips and uneven surfaces.

He let out an involuntary shriek when the toe of his shoe clipped the edge of one of the errant chunks of concrete.

"Eeee!" He was ashamed of himself even before his right knee hit the sidewalk. One leg back, the other bent below him, he held the stance of a track athlete getting his footing on the blocks. Three breaths while he assessed the damage, and then he looked up and knew his pride had taken more of a fall than his body.

"Are you alright?" asked a woman standing two feet in front of him. She held her hands over her mouth to contain her laughter. Or, at least, that's what Jeremy assumed. It wasn't until she reached down to help him up that he saw the look on her face wasn't one of amusement, but concern.

"Yeah, yeah I'm, uh—" He got his feet underneath him. Twenty-seven-years-old and only kissed two girls. The first was on a dare at a high school party he couldn't believe he allowed himself to attend. The second at the end of a date with a friend of a friend. He couldn't bring himself to dial the last 9 in her phone number after that. Now he searched for words like "I'm fine," or "thank you," to say to the woman on the sidewalk that had just helped him up, but no words came.

The woman waited for him to finish with the patience of a kindergarten teacher. Finally, Jeremy shrugged and said, "Good. I'm good."

But she didn't leave. He looked for a quick exit. He failed. "I'm Rachel," she said.

Should I shake her hand? He thought. *She already took my hand when she helped me up. Did that count? Would it be repetitive?*

Instead, he surprised himself by offering a quick bow and saying, "I'm Jeremy."

A bow?

He walked this street countless times but hadn't seen her before. He's confident he would have noticed her; long brown hair that wrapped around itself in loose curls, matching brown eyes so dark the pupils would go missing when her face fell into shadow, and even when concern tightened her face, a slight upturn on the ends of her thin lips. Jeremy couldn't turn away from her. She was beautiful—which stoked the need to flee.

"Do you work around here?" she asked.

"I work at—" Jeremy turned around to point to the office building down the road when the high-pitched squeal of tires sliding across pavement erupted. They whipped their heads toward the road.

A red sedan slid sideways across the yellow line and smoke erupted from the rear wheel well of a white van moving the opposite direction. The collision resounded in a low-pitched boom with a simultaneous high scratch. Jeremy covered his ears with his hands and turned away. The van's horn blared a single, elongated note that would continue until someone with technical know-how could pry open the hood and disconnect something-or-other.

People were drawn from surrounding businesses. A few heroic individuals walked up to the crumpled vehicles to see if they could help until an ambulance arrived. Jeremy looked over his shoulder and saw Rachel facing the accident with her hands again over her mouth.

The trance between them had been broken and even though his mind shouted at him to stay, his body retreated the way he came.

A week passed. His lunch breaks took him down the street with the overgrown tree to the diner on the corner except for Tuesday when it rained and he was forced to eat in the break room. He hated the break room and its fluorescent lighting. Too many coworkers. He was much happier when he could stroll along the sidewalk, scanning the faces of passersby for Rachel. Every day was a disappointment until he sat in the window seat at the diner on Friday.

"We got the club back today," said the waitress after he settled into the booth. "The soup?" he asked.

"Clam chowder."

He opened his mouth to speak—

"New England," she finished.

He nodded. "Sounds great. Thank you."

She disappeared without writing anything down.

Jeremy was the only person in the restaurant eating alone. He couldn't fathom having someone to watch him dribble soup from his chin before he could catch it with a napkin. He became overly sensitive to the sounds of chewing whenever he found himself in the unfortunate circumstance of sharing a meal with somebody. It was uncomfortable. It felt gross.

He happened to glance out the window as he crunched his second cracker into the half-finished bowl of soup. It was like a scene in a movie where the clouds parted, rays of sun beamed down like a spotlight, and harp music breathed from the speakers; Rachel stood just outside the glass.

The spoon clanked as he abruptly dropped his hands to the table. He looked around but nobody noticed. What should he do? Knock on the window? Go outside? Try to speak through the glass? The scene had been running through his mind for the last week like when a pop song haunts your every thought. But instead of singing one phrase over and over, he imagined what he would say to Rachel should they run into each other.

You know, I really fell for you last week. It's too bad someone crashed our party. Sorry I had to split.

But none of it felt right. He couldn't be like those guys on the TV shows. In reality, he'd probably just mumble until she grew bored. But at least he practiced for that scenario. Here behind the glass, he was at an extreme disadvantage and couldn't figure out—

She turned toward the glass. There was no reason for her to do it, but all the same, it happened. He watched as she adjusted her gaze from the reflection to what lay beyond: Jeremy. Her eyebrows jumped up. She smiled and waved.

Jeremy's heart increased its already rapid output and he waved back. Eye contact had always been difficult past an initial few seconds, so he diverted his glance to the empty seat next to him. *Get it together, wave to her or something.* He turned back and forced a smile. She nodded before he could raise his shaking hand. Then she walked to the diner's entrance.

Oh no, I think I just invited her in.

Panic flushed his limbs.

The bell on the door dinged and the hostess greeted her. Jeremy watched as Rachel said a few words and pointed to his table. He felt like his lottery number and draft number had been called at the same time.

"Hey Jeremy," she said.

The shock of her remembering his name briefly clouded his mind. She stood next to the table. He remained in his seat.

"Hi. Wanna sit?" he asked.

She smiled, nodded, and sat. She bounced a couple times to the middle of the seat. He liked that she didn't slide, though he wasn't sure why.

"That was pretty crazy last week, right? I mean, that accident was right next to us," she said.

He nodded. "Yeah. Pretty nuts."

"I must've lost you in all the hubbub."

"Well, it was a pretty hectic scene."

She paused. The eye contact between them felt like a tug-of-war but he forced himself to hold it.

And then the shaking started.

At first it was a dull rumble that rattled Jeremy's spoon inside the bowl. It began to dance along the rim before it shot across the puddle of soup and onto the table. By that time, it didn't matter because the bowl itself was dancing on its edges. Jeremy looked up and caught Rachel's eyes, this time wide open and frightened.

"Get under the table," he said.

They slid into their makeshift bunker and watched as people braced themselves against the counter. Stacks of plates in the kitchen shattered on the ground. Pots and pans banged together and sounded like ten people simultaneously playing different songs on steel drums.

People shouted. A baby cried.

"It's almost over," he said to Rachel. She nodded.

The shaking probably lasted six seconds. Eight tops. But it was strong. Jeremy and Rachel crawled back into their seats to find the restaurant around them absolutely trashed. Broken porcelain littered the floor. Food scraps and spilled drinks covered tables. Customers and workers alike looked around the café like they had unexpectedly teleported and were trying to figure out where they were.

"That was awful," said Rachel. She had been so sure of herself. The crack in her confidence emboldened Jeremy to fill it in.

"Was that your first earthquake?" he asked.

She nodded. "I moved here not too long ago. Give me a thunderstorm and I'm fine, but this—" She shook her head and left the sentence in the air.

"Alright," shouted one of the servers. "If you have an open bill, stay seated and we'll get everything square. Anybody who hasn't ordered, get out."

Jeremy looked back to Rachel. She shrugged.

"I should get back to work anyways," she said.

He watched as she delicately walked over shattered plates, cups, and bowls. The door dinged as she walked back into the afternoon.

He sighed and closed his eyes.

Five days passed. Jeremy had taken to walking through his lunch break instead of eating.

Granola bars at his desk sustained him just fine. His free hour in the midday was devoted to scanning the street for one particular set of eyes. Women weren't inexplicably drawn to him, yet Rachel seemed to be. Why? In the end, of course, the reason didn't matter. All that mattered was that there was a kind woman who enjoyed his company. Another unproductive lunch break left him with an afternoon of light snacks and an immovable distraction from his workload.

The sun had set by the time he walked out of the building that evening. The seasons were changing but luckily, the air was still warm. He decided to go against his routine and take one more walk around the neighborhood.

The night was unusually calm. Traffic seemed light. The streets were quiet. He walked along the sidewalk and gazed at the surrounding buildings in the downtown district. The town wasn't large, but if you sat on the sidewalk and gazed upwards, you could almost trick yourself into believing there was a skyline. The office buildings remained mostly lit. He glanced around, taking in the hidden beauty of the neighborhood and giving himself a break from thinking about Rachel.

"Jeremy?"

He brought his sights back to ground-level and saw her standing ten feet in front of him.

"Hey," he said. He released a deep breath and felt as if opening his eyes from a meditative state. His heart rate increased, but not much. "It's great out here tonight, isn't it?"

She glanced around. "It's easy to forget somebody actually built these things, y'know? They almost seem like they've always been here, or were built by robots. But a person, or a few of them, planned everything out and then other people used tools and machines to put them together." She slowly turned to take in more of the view.

He stepped toward her and she dropped her gaze back to him. The nerves sparked to life with every step he took. By the time he was within arm's reach, his legs shook at the knees. He wanted to hug her, to pick her up and protect her from all of life's nasty tendencies, but in reality, she was better suited to protect him. Instead, he stood there and looked into her eyes without turning away. It was the bravest thing he could think of at the moment.

And then the power went out.

All the streetlamps, all the illuminated offices within the buildings, every source of light besides the headlights from the occasional passing car was extinguished. Rachel gasped. It took a moment for Jeremy's eyes to adjust to the darkness. The moon and a few stars glistened above them, and after a moment it almost felt like a candlelit dinner. Intimate. Romantic. Private. A smile grew on his lips and he reached toward her, but she stepped back.

"You know, I'm not superstitious or anything, but this is really weird." She crossed her arms and glanced around at the dark storefronts and office windows. The street was oddly quiet; like they were the only people in the city.

"I like you," he said. It sounded like something a middle schooler would say, but at least he said something. "You're compassionate," he continued, "and kind. I want to learn more about you."

Her arms stayed crossed. "Every time we're near each other, a disaster happens."

"Maybe it's like Newton's third law. Equal and opposite reactions for every action. Maybe it's just the universe balancing itself out."

"By making bad things happen?"

"If bad things are happening to balance out our meeting, that has to mean our meeting is a good thing."

Silence surrounded them. Shadows dotted the sidewalk below them from the white glow of the moon from above. Jeremy could only see it after staring just to the side of the shadow below Rachel. It would disappear once he focused his attention on it. He looked back up and Rachel's arms had come loose. He stepped toward her and again extended his hands. This time, she took them.

"You know we could end the whole world, right?" she asked. Jeremy shrugged and turned his eyes to the sky above.

CHANCE TO FADE

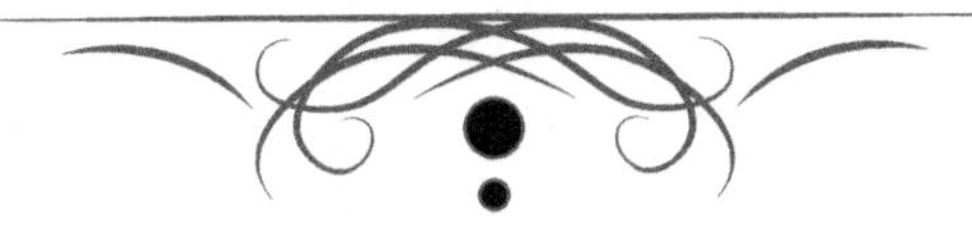

SATURDAY

"Let me guess, not much fun, right?"

David nodded as his brother sat down at the circular table, covered in an off-white linen that Fiona had chosen. They sat alone. They caught occasional glances from the surrounding crowd, the bravest of which offered terse condolences. The DJ's multi-colored lights bounced around the high-ceilinged room.

Michael set another plastic cup of beer in front of David. "I really can't believe they went through with this."

David shrugged. "Her parents are practical people. They paid for it, so on paper, it makes a lot of sense."

"Look at that DJ," Michael motioned with his beer. "He's a wedding DJ. He has no idea what he's doing."

David glanced from table to table, each filled by solemn guests chewing to avoid the need to speak. No one danced. David wondered if it would be any different if this were still the wedding reception Fiona had planned.

"People already had the flights booked, the hall was rented, catering, decorating—it was all taken care of. What were they supposed to do? Cancel it and do it all over again?"

"Dave, stop making sense of this." Michael grabbed his brother by the shoulder. "Have you gone back to work yet?"

David shook his head and it felt like he was underwater. He hadn't been keeping track of his drinks—not that anybody expected him to.

"You gotta go back to work. How long's it gonna take?"

David locked eyes with his brother and ignored the flashes of red, green, and blue that crossed his face. "I don't know. But definitely longer than three weeks." He turned his head toward the DJ booth. A table sat to the right that should be draped with off-white linen and topped with gift-wrapped packages. Instead, the DJ's lights swung festively over the exposed wood of the table with a singular urn at the center. Fiona.

David felt another squeeze on his shoulder and looked back at Michael, his younger brother. Unmarried. Twenty-eight. Same blond hair and same patchy beard as David. He remembered watching Michael scream at another kid when they were in high school because he called David fat. Watching Michael through the dancing DJ lights, he felt the same tightness in his chest as he did in the parking lot outside of school that afternoon.

A high-pitched and thin voice suddenly cut through the music that would have made sense at a reception, but seemed cruel at a wake. "Hi David."

He looked to his left. Emma, a girl from the apartment next door, climbed onto the chair beside him. She was the first person besides Michael to accept the commitment of sitting down beside the would-be husband and the near widower.

"What's happening?" she asked. Emma had as good a right as anyone to be invited to the wedding. For four years, David and Fiona agreed to occasionally spend an evening with her while her parents took a night off to go to a movie, or a restaurant, or anywhere they didn't have to watch their language. She was now ten years old, and although not old enough to be left alone, their services were only requested in the case of an emergency. The fact that her parents didn't seem to take time off could have indicated many things, but Fiona and David tried not to read into it.

"Just talking to my brother," said David as cheerily as he could. The beer helped.

"No, I mean what's happening here?" she said.

"What?"

"No one will tell me. What happened to Fiona?"

David sighed and looked over Emma's head, where her parents were speaking with another couple strangers. His face started to grow hot at the idea of someone being here that he didn't recognize, and then he remembered that he didn't have a stake in the day anymore.

Michael either hadn't heard her question or didn't care to involve himself. He instead scanned the room. David took another drink of his beer.

"Well," he said. "I didn't save her when I should have."

"What does that mean?"

"It means I shouldn't have let her walk to the store alone." Almost as bad as the fact that his fiancé had been killed, was the fact that he had lost her because he forgot to buy a box of pasta at the grocery store. He remembered the tomato sauce, the tomatoes themselves, the seasonings and the ground beef, but he neglected the pasta. Spaghetti gets its name from the spaghetti noodles but somehow it didn't cross his mind as he gathered ingredients for dinner.

Fiona had said she needed to take a walk anyway, so why not go to the end of the street and grab the noodles. David didn't see anything wrong with the idea at the time. He certainly did now.

"She was hit by a car," he said.

"She didn't look both ways?" asked Emma.

"Sometimes, looking both ways doesn't guarantee anything."

"Hey, is she talking your ear off?" Connor appeared above his daughter and started combing her shoulder-length brown hair with his fingers.

"No, no it's fine." Looking up at Connor made David feel more like Emma than her father, even though he and Connor were just about the same age.

Connor smiled and put his hand on Emma's shoulder. "Go find Mom. It's almost time to go."

"Bye David," she said without another glance in his direction. He watched as she jogged over to where her mother seemed to be stuck in conversation with a small group of unknown people.

Connor remained standing behind the chair. "She's a real handful," he said.

David agreed, even though his babysitting nights were never more difficult than watching a puppy. The music from the speakers on either side of the DJ booth was too loud but it was a nice break from silence.

"Did you guys make those brownies every time Emma came over?"

"What's that?"

"It seemed like every time we dropped her off at your place, she'd come home with a plate of brownies."

"I guess maybe. It was a good way to eat up time and Fiona was just so good at making them. I didn't do much more than wash the dishes."

Connor glanced down and smirked. "There was that one time you tried to make them."

David almost chuckled. "*Tried* is the operative word." He usually hated small talk. It was a waste of time. But wasting time was all he was able to do until he could finally leave without looking like he was throwing a tantrum. Another silence appeared between them.

Connor shook his head, pursed his lips, and raised his eyebrows. "You know about Allen, right?" His voice was quieter.

"Yeah." David remembered Emma asking why she had to brush her teeth but Allen didn't. *Because Allen doesn't have teeth,*

Fiona told her. They hadn't heard of Allen in a while and David thought he disappeared, but as the babysitting gigs became more infrequent, he didn't expect to have updated information.

Still shaking his head: "Well, he's back."

"Connor, c'mon," came a voice behind them.

Connor glanced behind himself. "Gotta run. Ball 'n chain."

David raised his cup as Connor walked over to his family, and finished it as he surveyed the scene around him. Everyone treated him like a leper. He didn't think they blamed him for the accident—he was doing a good enough job of that himself—but they didn't want to face him.

The contrast in expectation for the night versus the reality was too drastic. Wedding receptions are for raucous revelry, wakes are for calm reflection. And this was probably the first wake to include a DJ playing his standard wedding playlist, but at a slightly lowered volume. He saw Michael in line for another beer and became flushed. His face grew hot and he started sweating. If he had eaten any of the catered food, he would have been worried about vomiting, but luckily that wouldn't be an issue.

A word flashed through his mind: *FLEE*. It felt like a neon sign in his brain. Any concern about decorum vanished from his priority list. He quickly found his legs beneath himself and avoided eye contact as he walked between the rows of tables, through the gymnasium-style doors at the back of the room, down the hallway, and out of the automatic doors leading to the sidewalk.

The warm August night didn't do much for his flushed face, but the fresh air soothed the pain inside of his chest. The more he breathed, the better he felt, and he didn't stop walking. He briefly thought about his car in the parking garage behind him but then he remembered the untold amount of beers he'd had.

He made his way toward the apartment complex they had so recently shared, and slowed his stride once he realized what was going to be waiting for him once he got back there: An empty apartment filled wall-to-wall with memories that had been haunting him since she failed to make it through the crosswalk three weeks before.

Trees lined the sidewalk on the other side of the street. Beyond that, a park with a playground, abandoned beneath the moonlight. His thoughts flashed to the empty apartment for another moment before he crossed the street and found the swing set.

Wasting time isn't always such a waste. He sat on one of the rubber rectangles and felt the chains dig into his hips. The swing wasn't designed to carry a thirty-year-old man, but the links held as they creaked beneath his weight. He didn't care if the black dress pants ripped. He didn't care that he lost the suit coat an hour before somewhere in the rented hall. He kept hold of one of the support chains while he tore at his throat until his tie fell onto the woodchips below.

He couldn't remember the last time he sat on a swing and pumped his legs until momentum took control, and that was a good thing. Lately, all he could do was remember all the last times. He hoped that once her ashes were spread at her family's house on the lake up north where she'd spent her childhood summers, he could find a stopping point. A period on the sentence. A delineation between the life they shared together for five years and whatever would come after that. The wake was over, their wedding date would have passed, and he would be left with himself, his future, and his memories. And then his phone started ringing.

"Hello?" he said. Alone in the playground underneath a surprisingly bright moon, it felt like another planet.

"David? Where did you go?" asked Michael.

"I had to get out of there. I just, I had to."

"Well don't you think I would have liked to know that? You think I'm here to meet new people?"

"Yeah, I know. I'm sorry."

"Don't worry about it. Now I have an excuse."

David held the phone to his head and continued to swing.

"Alright, well, I'll stop by tomorrow, okay? Get some coffee before I go to work or something," said Michael.

"Yeah, sounds good."

He slid the phone back in his pocket and let his momentum fade until his feet slowly skidded across the woodchips. He left his tie next to the swing set and walked the rest of the way home trying, and failing, to think about the moon.

A streetlight stood directly in front of the entrance to the apartment building: A three-story complex with six units on each floor and a fire escape weaving a trail between the windows. He could see his bedroom window on the top floor, off to the left. The one directly to the right he knew to be Emma's. The building had a balance of charm and practicality that David described simply as "adult," even though Fiona thought it was an oversimplification mixed with a bit of projection. She might have been right, even though she used the same argument when she questioned David about his job. He thought of himself as an artist when they first met, but as he approached the end of his twenties, he felt he needed the classification of "adult" and landed an entry-level job cashing checks and checking balances at a local bank. Now, two years later, he had an "adult" job and an "adult" apartment but no one to share it with.

He looked at the light pole which used to be a favorite spot for one of the tenants to lock up a blue road bike. The bike found a new location to park after a stray cat, gray with black spots and a strangely white tail, died at the base of the light and had yet to be noticed by the city. That was a few months earlier and now the cat looked more like a frizzy oven mitt than a pet, and David couldn't help but look at it every time he came home or left.

He walked inside, rode the elevator to the third floor, and passed two doors before stopping outside the one labeled 304. He took two deep breaths and opened the door. He ignored the light switch and walked to the couch where he dropped his keys on the coffee table in front of him. He didn't need the light to avoid the dining table to his right, or to walk slightly to his left to avoid the side table and couch. He didn't need to see the kitchen off to the right, or the short hallway to his left. Their room, now simply his room, was to the right in the hallway. A small closet acted as the buffer between the bedroom and the bathroom at the opposite end of the hallway. The apartment wasn't small, but there also wasn't any space to waste.

The pillows, the dishes, the clothes—he didn't want to see, so he sat in the dark. A vague orange haze from the street lights crept through the blinds. His eyes adjusted to the dim light after a few moments. He could make out the TV in front of him, the pictures on the wall behind it. To his right, by the window, sat the potted plants. The one hanging from the macramé hanger which hadn't been watered since Fiona last pulled the stepstool from next to the refrigerator. He looked around his dark apartment until something didn't make sense. There was a shape in the corner opposite the plants, but along the same wall. It was as if he left out the vacuum cleaner, except it was a little bigger. It wasn't a coat and it wasn't a plant, and then his heart turned electric and his veins went cold.

"Who's there?" he yelled as he jumped from the couch. He punched his arm to the right and clumsily flicked on the standing lamp next to the couch. The figure he thought he saw through the dark was gone, most likely never there in the first place. "Jesus Christ," he said to himself as he walked over to the front door and flicked on the light switch. He locked the door, drank a glass of water, and went to bed but didn't fall asleep.

Emma ran her hands along her skirt but the seatbelt made it bunch up in weird ways. She hated that party. All she thought about was crawling into bed. There was just so much to say.

"Well, did you have fun sweetie?" Connor spoke over his shoulder as he rolled his window back up after paying the attendant in the little hut in the parking garage.

She shook her head but her dad wasn't looking.

"Emma?" he asked.

"Yes," she said mechanically.

The car pulled onto the road and into light traffic.

"I don't blame you," said Samantha. She turned to Connor. "Who does something like that? Just to save a few bucks? And it was like we had to go because of the RSVP and all that. Painfully awkward. *Painfully awkward.*"

Connor shrugged.

Emma watched the floor of the car in front of her. Her legs weren't long enough to reach the mats and the streetlights swooped across as they drove down the road. Her parents continued talking but Emma wasn't interested. She was imagining each flash of light as a being. A friend. Someone she could talk to that wouldn't call her names or make her feel scared. She'd rather hear what the beams of light had to say instead of her parents, but she knew she'd get in trouble if she tried to ask them if they were warm or cold. Inertia pushed her slightly forward as her dad eased up to a red light. Now she had new beams of light to befriend.

Two boys that were probably in high school but looked to Emma like full-fledged adults walked along the crosswalk in front of the car. Emma watched them and imagined Fiona doing the same thing, but not reaching the other side. A moment later, the light turned green and they made their way around a few more corners, through a few more stop lights, and into the parking garage below their apartment building. Emma thought about the cat by the streetlight and wondered if it didn't make it across the street like Fiona.

Connor went straight to the couch after walking into the apartment and flipped on the TV. The kitchen and small dining room sat directly inside the front door of the apartment, with the living room beyond that. On the right side of the apartment was a short hallway with the bathroom acting as door number one. Door number two was a closet and at the end of the hall sat the two bedrooms, doors number three and four, which forced the hallway into an L-shape.

Connor and Samantha kept their stuff behind door number three, and Emma often hid behind door number four. Connor sat on the couch in his nice clothes and let out a deep breath.

"Why don't you go brush your teeth, honey," said Samantha while Emma struggled to peel her shoes off her feet. Emma nodded. "I'm going to get out of this dress. I'll come say goodnight in a minute." Samantha's heels echoed off the hardwood floor as she made her way to door number three, and Emma walked toward door number one.

She paused after Samantha disappeared into her bedroom, and decided to skip the chore and go straight to bed. She didn't sneak past her mother, but she was careful not to make any noise.

She closed the door behind herself and flicked on the overhead light, which she never liked. It cast a sterile, white light on the room and made shadows basically non-existent. She preferred the soft, yellow glow of the lamp on the desk near the window which sent long shadows stretching across the floor and walls. She faced the window when she entered her room, which was bisected by her bed jutting out from the wall on the right. The bed seemed to point to the closet on the left wall, where, on the other side of which, her mother was changing clothes.

The wall between their bedrooms was thick and housed their closets. Emma could hear her mother hanging her dress in her own closet and often wondered how much they could hear from their side of the wall. She was perfectly comfortable in her dress and in no rush to change into her pajamas, so she opened her closet door but didn't walk inside. Instead, she stood just outside with her hand resting on the doorknob.

"Hello?" she said quietly. The overhead light illuminated the shallow closet and she could easily see her three pairs of shoes on the floor beneath the hanging clothes. The shelf above, which she needed help to reach, held a couple board games, some dolls she never named, and a hat that wouldn't be appropriate until frost appeared on the outside of her window. "Are you there?" she asked.

"What are you doing?" asked a voice from her left.

Emma jumped. She quickly swung her head toward the voice and saw her mom standing inside her bedroom door. She had one hand on her hip and the other on the doorknob.

"Nuh—nothing," said Emma.

"I thought I told you to brush your teeth."

"I was going to get pajamas like you," lied Emma. She did it often, but never thought of it as lying. In her mind, she was just finding easier ways to explain things.

Samantha looked at her for another moment before she finally nodded. "Change quick, then get those teeth brushed." She walked into the living room where Emma could hear her talking to Connor. Emma quickly crawled out of her dress and into the pants that weren't quite sweatpants and the shirt that was like a normal t-shirt but softer. She walked down the hallway and into the bathroom where she grabbed her toothbrush from under the sink. She hit it with a little water, put some toothpaste along the bristles, and got to work. She felt her father's fingers running through her hair before she had taken her first spit break.

"Getting tired, Emma?" he asked.

She spit. "Why don't some people stop at red lights?" she asked. Toothpaste colored the sides of her mouth like blue chalk.

Connor stopped smiling and looked down at her. "What?"

"I thought the lights were the boss?" She held the toothbrush in her hand and looked up at him.

"They—uh—they are sweetie." His eyes shifted toward the living room.

"Well not when Fiona was walking." Emma heard footsteps coming down the hallway. "What was that?" asked Samantha from outside the bathroom.

"Fiona's light was green, wasn't it?"

Samantha moved into the doorframe, forcing Connor near the toilet. "Who told you that?" Then, to Connor: "Did you tell her that?"

"No," he said. "I didn't tell her anything."

"Nobody tells me anything," Emma said quietly.

"What was that?" asked Samantha.

"Nothing." Emma rinsed her toothbrush, rinsed her mouth, and turned toward her mother. "Excuse me."

Samantha looked from Emma to Connor and stepped aside.

"I can't believe you told her that," said Samantha as Emma walked past her. Their words followed her down the hall.

"I didn't say anything."

"We talked about this."

"I didn't *say* anything."

"Well somebody certainly did and I know it wasn't me."

Emma closed the bedroom door behind her and listened to her parents' muffled voices for a moment. The door usually erased the exact words they said, but the exact words weren't all that important. The inflections and volume were enough to give her a general feeling of the tone of the conversation. Emma turned off the overhead light and walked through the dark to her desk where she clicked on the lamp. The yellow light immediately replaced the soft, vague orange glow from the streetlight outside unless she looked at her window. The streetlight was almost directly outside but it could be drowned out with a light from within. She wished she could do the same with noise. Even the humming of a small fan would be enough to drown out the muffled discussion which still seemed to be taking place in the bathroom.

She crawled into her bed and pulled the covers over herself despite the heat. She enjoyed the light hug it afforded her and even tucked her feet inside. The closet door was still open but now she couldn't see the hanging clothes, shoes beneath, or board games above. For all she knew, they no longer existed. The lamp to her right cast the shadow of the wall from the right side of the closet's door frame almost all the way to the left. With the back of the closet obscured, it looked like the entrance to a secret tunnel or a cave. And even though she knew the wall was only about three feet back, this was how she thought of the closet at night. Most kids might be afraid of the unknown parts of a dark closet, inventing monsters and other ghoulish creatures that would nibble on their toes as they slept. Emma found it comforting. She always slept with her light on, but not because she was afraid of the dark. She was afraid of missing something.

"Goodnight," she said to her closet.

SUNDAY

Shadows evaporated from the receding dark as the sun came up. Traces of the night clung to the wall in small patches behind the dresser and on the floor beside the bed. He hadn't moved for hours. No turning. No fidgeting. He lay in bed alternately closing and opening his eyes with the exasperation of the insomniac. The mind turned too quickly and frequently. The envelope of sleep never had a chance to close. This would make two nights in a row of pure sleeplessness.

Since Fiona's accident, sleep had become difficult but attainable. At least in short bursts. But now, as the intensity of the sunshine through the window grew, he would begin his third day on the reserve of one bad night of sleep.

He'd grown accustomed to the silence and stillness of the apartment so when the knock came through the front door it sounded like the fist of God trying to break into hell. He jerked upright as if prodded by an electrical shock and almost fell as he rolled off the bed. He padded to the door and tried to calm his breathing. He knew who it was once the lightning in his head had a chance to fade. With two clicks the door was unlocked and opened.

"You look terrible," said Michael.

"Good morning to you, too." David stepped aside and Michael walked into the apartment. "You didn't need to Tyson my door."

"Figured I'd have to wake you up."

"Figured wrong."

Michael glanced around the apartment like he hadn't been there a hundred times already. "It just looks so—the same."

Without her, was the part he left off. David agreed, even though it didn't really mean anything.

"Come on. Put some clothes on and let's get a coffee."

David nodded and did as he was told. Five minutes later he was locking the door to his apartment. They rode the elevator to the ground floor and walked outside. The sun was up but not too far. It would still be another few hours before the seasonal heat would become irrefutable. At this point, with joggers still cramming it in before work and dogs getting their after-breakfast relief, one could still lie to himself and say, *Maybe it won't feel like an oven today.* But that would be wrong.

"It looks like someone forgot their hand puppet," Michael said and motioned to the cat lying next to the light post.

"I hate that you're right," said David.

They walked along the sidewalk for a couple blocks before taking a right and stepping into a small café. Red metal chairs surrounded three red metal tables out front, and a sandwich-style chalkboard sign contained a daily pun to catch the roamer's attention. Michael loved it. David hated it. Today it said: *Beat the grind and espresso yourself!*

"How about you David? How are you going to espresso yourself today?" Michael asked as they pushed their way through the glass door. The aroma of sugar-covered pastries and fresh ground coffee engulfed them. David took in a deep breath and ignored his brother's stupid question.

"Take a seat," said David. "I'll get us some coffees."

"Hey, I'm the one who's been going to work." They spoke as they walked to the short line. "Speaking of which, how long can you put that off?"

"Put what off?"

"Going back to work."

David sighed. Work. He couldn't even sleep. Focusing on anything more intricate than a passing conversation with his brother seemed impossible.

"Listen, man. I don't mean to be so blunt but someone's gotta say it. She's dead. Okay? I know you guys were this close to being married but at some point you gotta let her go."

"Can I, um, help you?"

David and Michael turned to the woman behind the register. She bit her bottom lip on the right side and bounced her glance from one brother to the other.

"You mean with an order, right?" asked Michael.

She nodded slightly.

"Yeah, we'll take two twelve-ounce blends and an apple cinnamon muffin," said David. "Thanks."

Michael won the race to his wallet and paid. A moment later, David grabbed the coffees, Michael picked up the plated muffin, and they walked to a table toward the back of the café. It wobbled as David set the coffees down, but it was impossible for them to avoid spilling so he didn't pay it any attention.

A month earlier, David and Fiona sat near the front window of the café at a sturdier table. They made somewhat of a ritual out of walking up there on Sunday mornings, splitting whatever pastry looked the most decadent, and sharing a large cup of coffee.

"How many nuclear bombs do you think we have?" she asked on their last Sunday at the café.

"Unless you're hiding some in the back of the closet, I think I have a couple under the sink."

"Close to ten grand. There aren't even two hundred countries. We have about fifty nuclear bombs for each country."

"That seems like almost enough." David took a drink of the coffee and set it back in the middle of the table. "So is there a giant underground silo in Nebraska or something? Packed to the roof with nukes?"

"Funny you should ask. The largest stockpile is actually twenty miles from Seattle. In the ocean."

David opened his mouth to make a joke about glowing fish.

"And it's guarded by dolphins." Fiona sat back and crossed her arms, smirking like she just won a game of checkers.

"What?"

She leaned forward, arms still crossed. "Navy-trained dolphins."

But now, David and his brother settled themselves on opposite sides of the wobbly table and the conversation was a little less light-hearted.

"So, it's over, right?" said Michael. "Her ashes are going to be spread, and it's done."

"I was thinking along those same lines last night, actually."

"So I'm right?"

David took a drink of his coffee and burnt his tongue. After forcing himself to swallow and feeling the burning gulp absorb into his chest, he said: "I hope so."

"Did they say how long of a furlough you could take? The bank?"

"We saved so much for the wedding. We put it in my savings because she didn't have any self-control when it came to spending. And then her parents went ahead and paid for it all. Surprised the hell out of us."

"I guess that's why they didn't want to just throw it all away last night."

"Yeah, I guess so." David tried his coffee again and it was still too hot, but not as bad as before. One more drink and he would acclimate to the heat. He took it. The next drink was almost near pleasant. He grabbed the edge of the muffin, tore it off, and shoved it into his mouth. "But that job. That's not a fun job."

"And you think I enjoy rolling forward the pre-paid account sub-ledger?" Michael had yet to touch his cup.

David shrugged as he took another drink of coffee. Accounting didn't seem too far off from banking until Michael showed him a couple spreadsheets. His vision went blurry as his brother explained algorithms and columns.

"I didn't become an accountant because I enjoy it. I did it because I'm good at it. Work and play are not synonymous. There's a reason for that."

"I just—I got the job for Fiona, for her parents really, and now I don't see a point."

"So you wanna get a job at a movie theater or something? Pump gas? Wash dishes?"

"Nobody gets paid to pump gas anymore."

"They do in Oregon." Michael finally took a drink of his coffee. A voice cut through the din of the café: "Hey!"

They both looked toward the register where Connor was waving to them. David and Michael waved back.

Connor looked toward the line, a little longer now, and gave a quick shake of his head before walking over to their table. They again said their hellos.

"Hey, uh, great party last night." Connor stuck his hands in his pocket for a moment and took them right back out again. "I mean, y'know, it was nice."

"Sure, yeah. Thanks," said David.

"Could I ask you something? Did you tell Emma about Fiona?"

David nodded as he took another slow drink of coffee. It was lukewarm now.

"I really wish you wouldn't've. You know her. She's just so, I don't know, fragile? We really shouldn't be putting images and thoughts like that into her head." Connor stood next to the table and crossed his arms. David looked up at him.

"Well, it's the truth. Believe me, Connor, I wish it wasn't. But this is the world we live in and I'm not going to lie about her. To anybody."

Connor's pretzel-arms loosened and he nodded with tight lips. "Right. You're right," he said. "Look, David, I'm so sorry about all of this."

"Hey," said Michael as he nodded toward the front counter. "The line's empty."

Connor followed Michael's nod and said, "Oh. Yeah. Okay, well, I'll see you guys around."

"See you around, Connor," said David. He finished his coffee and took another bite of the muffin. He watched Connor get a couple coffees in paper cups and a muffin in a brown bag before retreating through the glass doors. He didn't wave goodbye. They listened to the standard café noise of clinking plates, indiscernible conversations, and the occasional drone of a coffee grinder for a couple minutes.

"You ready to get outta here?" asked Michael. David stood up.

They stayed mostly silent on the walk back to the apartment besides David thanking his brother for the coffee and muffin. Their reversed direction afforded a view of the intersection at the opposite end of the block. The side street came to a T and offered three crosswalks between the corners. The opposite corner from them housed the market where Fiona had planned to buy pasta. The crosswalk leading there was as far as she made it. He was baffled that he had walked across that same street the night before and hadn't realized the significance of it.

He realized they stood at the front of his apartment complex and he quickly pulled his keys from his pocket. Soon, they were in and out of the elevator, through his door, and standing inside the apartment.

"I gotta get going. To work," said Michael.

"Okay."

"You know, a leave of absence can't last forever."

"I know."

David tossed his keys onto the coffee table and sat on the couch. He looked over at his brother.

"You gonna be okay here?" asked Michael.

"Yeah, yeah, I'll be fine."

"What are you gonna do all day?"

David looked to the TV, then the window to his right, then into his lap as if a book or computer might have magically appeared. Seeing nothing, he looked back to Michael and shrugged.

"You gotta find something. You'll go crazy just sitting here. Start drawing again or something. Find a hobby."

"Yeah, maybe."

"Yeah, maybe," mimicked Michael. He grabbed the doorknob. "Alright, see you later." David responded with a wave as Michael closed the door behind himself.

The apartment was silent. He thought about the night and how he was able to pass hours in silence with hardly even moving. Could he do that on the couch during the day? Just pass the time waiting for the sun to set or alternately the sun to rise? He wanted something to change, but he couldn't bring himself to make it happen. The sun would inevitably change by the simple nature of the world spinning. If nothing else, at least he could count on that.

He stood up. Waiting for the sun to give way to the moon was no accomplishment and not worth waiting around for. He paced from the living room into the kitchen back into the living room down the hall and into the bedroom then back toward the living room. He ended up next to the couch, where he started. With a sigh, he sat back down and grabbed his laptop from the shelf below the coffee table. Maybe he could distract himself with world news or a science article or something. Movies were too long to hold his interest and TV shows were just stupid. It took a minute for the computer to boot up and he clicked the internet icon. A moment later, his home screen appeared along with a notification for an unopened email. Most likely, he thought, a message from work. He clicked on the highlighted icon and paused. The message didn't have a sender. This would usually indicate a scam of some sort and it would immediately be deleted, but in his sleep-deprived state, he accepted it as fact and opened it. There was no advertisement. No pornographic images. No chain mail request and no solicitation for action. There was one sentence with no signature and no greeting:

there is no future

"No," said Emma.

"When I was your age, I couldn't wait for the school year to start. New clothes, new friends—" Samantha let the last word hang in the air between them. They sat at the kitchen table, Emma with a glass of juice and Samantha with a glass of water. Connor left ten minutes earlier and should be back any minute. The café wasn't far.

Emma just shook her head.

"Is it the boys? The homework?" Samantha's voice grew a half-note higher and a little more forceful than was appropriate for breakfast.

Emma again shook her head and heard the key in the door.

"A little help here?" Connor said as the door swung open. A drink carrier dangled from one hand while the other clasped both a white bag and the keys. Emma took a drink of orange juice and looked to her mom, who first returned her gaze and then turned toward the door.

"Cool. Thanks." Connor dropped the keys on the ground and kicked them into the apartment. He walked inside, swung the door shut with his elbow, and placed the carrier and bag on the kitchen table. "They were out of apple cinnamon," he said to Emma. "So I got you blueberry. Okay?"

Samantha popped the tops of their coffees and unsheathed the muffin. Connor sat in the chair across from Emma, to Samantha's right.

Emma peeled into the warm muffin. Even at ten years old, she knew a singular muffin wasn't really a breakfast but it was sugary and delicious. Pretty soon, the summer mornings with no stress and no social navigation would be over. Her stomach turned to ice whenever she remembered school was only a couple weeks away. She held the muffin in two hands and felt like she had to unhinge her jaw like a snake to get a full bite. Her nose touched the top when she brought her teeth together.

It's quiet. No one's drinking their coffee. A minute passed before Connor finally spoke. "Emma, sweetie? How are you doing?"

She responded with a thumbs up and continued chewing.

"Good, good." Connor nodded his head. "I think, well *we* think, that it might be nice if you found some people your age to hang around with, y'know?"

"What?" asked Emma.

"Remember how you and Becky Roseland used to play together?" asked Samantha. "I remember finding you two with doll hair all over the floor when you decided they should all get new haircuts, remember?"

Emma nodded.

"We spoke with her mom and we think it'd be nice if we all went to the park today." Samantha slid her paper cup of coffee to the side as steam continued swirling from the top.

Emma sat back in her chair. "I don't like her anymore."

"But you two used to be friends," said Connor. "And I'd think you'd want to be there for her after her dad's accident."

Emma looked between her parents. Truth was, after they had gotten a couple years into school, Becky found some girls she liked more than Emma. It hadn't been Emma's choice to stop being friends. That fact was made very clear to her.

"I don't like her anymore," repeated Emma.

Samantha exhaled. "You don't like anybody," she said quietly.

"Hey," said Connor. "Ease up." Then, to Emma: "Why not?"

Emma shifted in her seat. She didn't like being in trouble. She was getting good at bending the truth but only when it was absolutely necessary. Sitting in front of her parents with a half-eaten muffin between them, she realized she didn't have a reason to lie.

"She's mean," she replied.

"To you?" Samantha leaned forward and rested her elbows on the table.

Emma wanted to tell them that Becky had grown a habit of hurting her on the playground during recess. That this was how Becky had gotten all of her new friends. They liked to talk and laugh and speak up in class and since Emma remained mostly quiet, she was called names.

A failure to retaliate makes a great target, but Emma didn't put that together. All she saw were the insults. The anger that replaced kindness. And the majority had to be right, right?

Maybe she was stupid. Maybe she was ugly. Maybe she deserved being thrown into the fence, or having her books slapped out of her hand, or having her chair pulled out from under her.

The majority of Emma's interaction with the world was through school, so how could she not extrapolate the schoolyard to the rest of society? She liked her parents, her neighbors, and that was about it. They were the only people that had an unbroken track record of acting in her best interests. Everybody else was suspect.

And now she was supposed to spend time with the same girl that had hit her in the back of the head with an ice ball the previous winter. But even if Emma didn't have a reason to lie to her parents, she also didn't have a reason to tell them the whole truth. They didn't need to know their daughter was a loser. She couldn't handle being viewed through that lens at home, too. So instead of explaining, she shrugged.

"Emma, you can talk to us. Don't just shrug us off," said Samantha.

"She's not shrugging us off," said Connor. "Just—just give her a second."

"Could you not?" she said to him.

Emma reached forward and grabbed the remains of her muffin, nearly crumbs at this point, and wrapped it in the stump paper. She climbed down from her chair, walked into the kitchen, and threw it away. She walked past the table on the way to her bedroom when Samantha suddenly spoke up.

"Honey?"

Emma paused and looked at her.

Samantha leaned forward and rested her elbows on her knees. "Are you still talking to Allen?"

"Oh Jesus Christ I thought we said we weren't going to bring that up," said Connor.

Samantha didn't move. "I saw you looking into your closet again. Was he in there?"

"Samantha, stop. There's nothing wrong with having an imaginary friend. Plenty of kids have them."

Samantha straightened up and turned around. "Yeah but plenty of kids also have real living friends, too. Dr. Chamberlain said that if she gets too detached it could lead to social development problems."

"Right in front of her? Come on, Samantha."

This wasn't the first time Emma heard terms like "social development problems" no matter how secretive her parents thought they were.

Samantha turned back to Emma. "It's okay, Emma. You can tell us if he's still there."

The silence felt weighted. A heavy blanket of expectation grew and her parents' eyes placed it directly over her head. Emma bounced her attention between them—their faces rigid. She thought of when they listened to the last big lottery numbers being called.

"No," she lied.

Connor nodded. "See? There you go."

The silence between sentences was suddenly punctured by a phony metallic jingling.

Connor said something under his breath and pulled his phone from his pocket. There were a few quick sentences before he slid it back in.

"I gotta go in early," he said. "Someone didn't do something or someone didn't come in, I don't know. But I gotta go." He stood up and clipped the lid on his coffee.

Emma walked into the hallway but stopped before she got to her room. After the sound of her footsteps disappeared, she could hear her parents in the kitchen.

"No, we're not going to bring that up. Not yet," said her dad's disembodied voice. "Chamberlain said only if it's drastic. It's not drastic."

"If there's a way for my child to stop being so uncomfortable all the time, I'm willing to give it a try."

"Me too, Sam. Me too. But being a kid is weird. All they know is everybody around them and they don't know anything. They fill in the gaps with emotions they can't control. Don't you remember what it's like? Did you ever screw up in front of a group of classmates? It feels like the world is going to end."

"This isn't fear. This is distrust. She doesn't trust anything or anybody besides us. Is that the bedrock of personality you want for your daughter?"

Emma walked into her bedroom and closed the door. Her parents didn't understand her.

Not as well as Allen did, at least. She climbed into her bed and her parents' voices faded to indistinguishable blobs. The morning sun cast small shadows across her wall and she stared at them, memorizing them. Then she said:

"Allen? Are you there?"

A few moments passed. A small shadow along the left edge of a picture frame on the wall opposite her bed shifted. First it ballooned on the top and then the enlargement slid to the bottom. After it gathered the whole of the shadow at the bottom corner of the frame, it jumped toward the closet and disappeared behind the door. A moment later, it jumped back to the edge of the frame.

Emma smiled.

David knew the internet was senseless, but he couldn't help puzzling over the messages. How does an email not have a sender? He had received countless spam emails but even if from a robot, they at least had a dummy account as a source. He stared at the four words longer than his eyes would let him focus. After a couple minutes, the sentence was nothing more than four blurry shapes on the computer screen and he had to shake his head to bring himself back to reality. Warm, quiet apartment. Summer heat still rising. Desperately alone.

The coffee sloshed in his stomach. Half of a muffin was not enough to balance out the warm liquid. The caffeine overpowered it. He and Fiona used to call it *The Fear*—shaky hands, a feeling of impending doom, and an inability to still one's thoughts. The mysterious email could certainly have a part in the anxiety growing within him, but coffee was a more concrete, and therefore resolvable, cause. He set the computer on the table, stood up, and walked into the kitchen.

Grocery shopping hadn't been much of a concern since Fiona took her last trip to the store. He certainly hadn't bought any noodles. There were still a few slices of bread, however, which he took out and set on a plate. A little mayonnaise, a slice of cheese, some soft lettuce that had yet to darken, and sliced turkey hiding behind the milk. He cut the sandwich in half and sat back on the couch. The TV came to life but the channels only offered overly happy news anchors trying to cook, game shows which were too flashy and overwhelming, and old sitcoms that stopped being relevant years before. He clicked the TV off and sat in silence, slowly munching on the sandwich.

His thoughts rewound to his morning with Michael. He had said to go back to work, which was definitely not going to happen today. He also said David should find a way to occupy himself. Find a hobby. Looking around the living room, his only other option seemed to be slowly devolving into a sleep-deprived madness so a hobby sounded like a good idea. He stood from the couch and walked into the bedroom.

He confronted Fiona's clothes in the closet and pushed them to the left. Still holding the plate, he reached for a box that had been stuffed in the corner for a year. He didn't know exactly what was inside, but he knew it was full of random stuff that didn't have any other place in the apartment. He grabbed it by a flap and it hung nearly on its side as he pulled it from the closet. The contents shifted but nothing reported a clink of fragility. He set it on the ground, shoved the rest of the sandwich in his mouth, set the plate on the nightstand behind him, and opened the box.

He found decorations Fiona had bought but never set up. A macramé plant hanger that never got paired with an eye hook laid across the top like a beached jellyfish. He pushed it aside and dug through folders which probably held birth certificates, social security cards, and copies of leases. Nothing of interest. There were forgotten Christmas decorations, an instruction manual for an old router, and finally a hardcover sketchbook with bent aluminum rings lining the spine. His name was on the cover, written in the scrawl of a college-age self that felt like two lifetimes ago.

He sat on the floor with his legs crossed and opened the book in his lap—pencil-shaded portraits of old friends on each page. They didn't appreciate the surreptitious pictures he used to take of them sleeping in class, eating in the cafeteria, or walking down the sidewalk, but David didn't care. Posed pictures were terrible. No one actually stood like that. So he'd print these pictures out and draw them. He thought they were the most true-to-life view of who they were, which he could internalize and convey on paper. Anna, John, Joseph—he hadn't seen them in years. Each page transported him to another lifetime, years before he met Fiona.

Summers spent on a stool with an easel and a sign for five dollar caricatures at city festivals. He put himself through art school with loans, but the summers of drawing people with exaggerated features kept his skills sharp and bolstered his bank account. It was the only time he made any money. Sure, he dreamed of making it into a career but life soon shook him into reality. He would have to draw fifty of these things a day, every day, to make anywhere near a respectable living. It didn't add up.

When he met Fiona a few years out of school, she took up the task of encouraging this dream. She loved his artistic side, but the struggles made him feel like an old man with a backwards hat. He felt a need to get a job that wouldn't embarrass him at high school reunions, so he submitted a resume to the local bank. Years passed, he climbed a few positions, and now he spent his days helping people sign up for credit cards and securing loans. Looking through the sketchbook in his lap, he tried to remember how it felt to enjoy work. He couldn't.

He pushed the box toward the closet but didn't go to the hassle of putting it back. He stood up, sketchbook in hand, and walked to the kitchen where he found an old pencil at the back of the junk drawer. His blood thudded through his veins. He might have felt excitement, but couldn't be sure. It had been a while. He fell backwards onto the couch, set the sketchbook on the coffee table, and flipped to the first blank page.

Now what?

The adrenalin that carried him here hadn't taken the necessity of an idea into account.

Something to bring to life. What could he draw? His recent thoughts were nothing but the crushing reality of an empty apartment surrounded by blame. There was no point in mining that when avoidance was the whole point.

It had been a few nights since he had a dream, but he remembered it clearly. It seemed to occur in real time. It was summer. People walked around the neighborhood in shorts and David walked down the road to a public pool that didn't actually exist.

He could feel the sun's heat and his body's thirst for cool moisture. He imagined his sweat as his body salivating for the big drink of submersion. He walked faster, which only made him warmer. Finally, he reached the pool and was just about to climb into the deep end when he saw something small land in the water in front of him. It was like a raindrop, but lighter. More gentle. He slowly lifted his gaze and saw snow falling from invisible clouds while the sun continued its assault on the world below. The snow landed on his exposed shoulders and was cold to the touch, but quickly melted. He woke up before he could get into the pool.

It wasn't the type of scenario he was accustomed to drawing, but it had been years since the portraits. It would be strange to reassume the exact habits of his younger self. The idea was to move forward even if the first step was small and private.

He leaned forward and put pencil to paper. He started by sketching the outline of the pool and after the first thirty seconds, it became a frenzy. There was nothing in the apartment besides the paper and the pencil. The walls and furniture along with his body and mind disappeared as the machinery of his arm and hand took over.

People appeared along the pool, some more in the water. Lounge chairs with rubber straps instead of cushions were placed along the edge. The cartoon-like quality of the caricatures was gone, replaced with the indiscriminate reality of the portraits. Except this time, the scope extended to cracks in the concrete, the reflection of sunshine off the waves in the water, and the beads of sweat that dotted every forehead that wasn't enjoying the relief of the pool.

And after the summer scene had been laid out in full, he peppered the page with snowflakes. Small, but distinguishable, there was only one person off to the side that looked into the air with a surprised expression. In order to avoid including himself in the picture, he drew the witness as a little girl. Self-exploration was not to be a feature of the drawing.

Altogether, he drew for half an hour. He set the pencil down, sat back into the couch, and took a deep breath. He felt like he had taken a nap. His heart danced in his chest and he felt as close to good as he had since the accident. Michael was right. He rubbed his face and took another couple deep breaths. He opened his eyes to look again at the drawing and was surprised at how clear everything was. Somehow, not only had there been no evidence of rust, but he seemed to have gotten better. The frenzy in which it was created felt so disembodied, it might as well have been drawn by somebody else. This gave him the ability to appreciate it as an outsider, despite the fact it had poured out of him moments earlier. He looked at the snowflakes in particular, and it seemed as if he had taken the time to create tiny shapes instead of simply dabbing the pencil a hundred times. He studied the waves and reflected sunlight when something in the corner of the room caught his eye. It was in the same spot as the figure from the night before. The figure that wasn't a vacuum cleaner or a coat.

The heartbeat that previously felt pleasant turned into a war drum and he snapped his head to the side.

Nothing.

He felt someone staring into him, but there was no one there. He stood up and walked toward the corner as if he had a chance of seeing footprints or any other proof of a bystander. But there was nothing. He needed sleep. He knew it. Hallucinations were never a sign of proper mental health, and he was scaring himself.

The apartment was quiet for about a half hour after Connor left for work. Emma heard the occasional footstep and one side of a short, muted conversation in the living room, but nothing else. She didn't say anything to Allen, and Allen didn't say anything back. Finally, there was a light knock on her bedroom door and it cracked itself open.

"Emma?"

"Yeah Mom."

Samantha stuck her head in the bedroom. "Get dressed. Let's go to the park."

Emma sighed and crossed one leg over the other. Her head rested on the pillow.

"I'm tired."

"Emma, it's the middle of the day and you're a kid. You need to get outside and play once in a while." She pushed the door fully open and stepped inside. "Plus, we have to meet the Roselands there in twenty minutes."

"The who?" Emma sat up.

Samantha offered a tentative smile. "Becky and her mom. I just got off the phone with her. They said they'd love to meet us there."

"No she didn't."

"Yeah. Come on. Look outside. It's beautiful today."

Emma looked at the window and the sunshine felt like a searchlight.

"We're leaving in ten minutes. You can go in your pajamas if you want to, but I'd recommend shorts." Samantha closed the door as she backed into the hallway.

The summer was almost over. Emma had to soak up her bedroom as much as possible before walking back into school. It was uncomfortable. Toxic. And nothing more was toxic than Becky Roseland.

There was nothing more dangerous than an enemy that used to be a friend. Becky knew about the time Emma wet her pants when they were playing hide and seek. And the time she started crying at a sleepover because she felt so homesick she might throw up. These memories eclipsed the times they laughed and played together. And now her mother had set up another afternoon where Becky could get more ammunition to use against her over the school year.

She wished for a lock on her bedroom door. She wanted to pile everything she had in front of it. But that wasn't an option. The only thing she could do was crawl out of bed, change out of her pajamas, and walk into the living room where Samantha was tying her shoes.

"Fine," said Emma. Her arms hung at her sides like dead animals.

Samantha, sitting on the couch and hunched over her shoes, looked up at her and smiled. "Great. This is going to be great."

They took the elevator to the parking garage in the basement, found the car, and pulled onto the road. Emma rolled down her window, stuck her arm outside, and realized her mom was right: It was a beautiful day. The sun was shining but someone must have turned down the thermostat a little because her skin didn't feel like it was near a flame. She tried to focus on the pleasant warmth of the day instead of worrying over the coming afternoon, but it was pointless.

The park was fairly close to their apartment building and her daydreams stole away the few precious moments she had to prepare. Samantha parked the car along the curb and Emma slowly pushed the door open. She sat there, not climbing out, until her mom walked around the car and looked at her.

"One leg out. Then the other," she said.

Emma sighed and did as she was told. The sound of her closing car door attracted the attention of two people, one old and one young, that stood beside a wooden picnic table about 20 yards into the park. Samantha waved at them. The old one waved back. Emma followed her mom toward the two and as they approached, the details obscured by distance slowly grew more crisp.

Becky's mom wore black leggings, a blue tank top, and had her hair in a ponytail. She looked as if she were about to go for a jog but Emma knew Samantha would have nothing to do with it. Becky stood next to her mom with her arms crossed. Blue jean shorts. A loose-fitting white shirt. She stared at Emma as she approached, but her face wasn't as hard as it had been throughout the past school year. Usually, she alternated between two expressions when dealing with Emma; either a rigidity saturated with disdain, or a condescending smirk. But today, she simply watched Emma as if she were a wild animal that had a chance of wandering near. She looked bored enough to maybe, possibly, be somewhat close to nice.

"Hey Emma," said Becky's mom. Then to Samantha: "Glad you guys could make it out. Feels like I haven't seen you in forever!"

"Well you know," said Samantha. "Things get a little crazy sometimes." Then to Becky: "Hi Becky. How's your summer going?"

"Almost over," she replied.

"Right." Samantha put her hand on Emma's back. "Why don't you two go play while us geezers talk about multivitamins and Medicare."

Becky's mom laughed.

Becky shrugged and walked into the playground behind them. Emma followed her. She heard Becky's mom start talking as they walked away.

"So tell me about this neighbor of yours? I heard someone got killed?"

The playground wasn't large. There were some stairs attached to a slide going one way and a bridge going the other. Monkey bars branched off the end of the bridge. A small swing set sat ten feet to the side. Becky walked to the swings and sat down. Emma sat next to her, on the same swing David, her neighbor, rode the night before. Becky pushed off and half-heartedly pumped her legs. Emma sat still.

A couple minutes passed without a word spoken. Emma looked around the park and counted squirrels. She only saw three.

"Aren't you going to swing?" asked Becky. "I feel dumb just doing it by myself." Emma looked up, nodded, and pushed off.

"Here, let's try to match up," said Becky.

Emma pumped a little harder and Becky leaned in the opposite direction to slow down and soon they were swinging directly next to each other. They remained silent, but being next to Becky without worrying about being taunted or pushed felt good. The absence of malice was close enough to affection for her.

"Why did your mom call my mom?" asked Becky. Emma shrugged. "I don't know."

"Is your mom lonely or something? I heard your parents fight a lot."

"No, they don't," said Emma. She didn't yell, but she wanted to.

"Hey, okay, jeez. I was just trying to make conversation. This is so boring."

Their tandem swing started to loosen a bit. It wasn't broken, but they weren't in perfect sync anymore.

"My neighbor died," offered Emma.

"Really?" Becky looked directly at Emma. "Yeah. Crossing the road."

"Wow," said Becky, dragging out the vowel.

Emma knew exploiting Fiona was dirty, but she desperately wanted the focus off herself. "Did you know him?"

"Her. And yeah, I did. She used to—" Emma paused, not wanting to use the term *babysit*. "Make me brownies."

"What's it like to know someone who's dead?"

"I thought it would be weirder. But it's just like she moved away. I mean, I didn't see what happened. It was just like one day she was there, and the next day, she wasn't."

They swung back and forth a few times in silence.

"Hey, do you wanna do an up-and-under?" asked Becky.

"Um, okay."

"Okay, you do me first and then I'll do you."

Emma nodded and skidded her feet in the woodchips until she stopped. She stood up and walked around the back, just out of reach of where Becky continued to swing. She started loosely pushing Becky's back to figure out the timing. One. Two. Three.

And then she went for it. With two hands on Becky's back, she ran forward and ducked her head. She felt Becky rise above her and heard a shout of excitement.

With her head still lowered, she brought her hands down and felt her finger latch onto something. Her momentum carried her forward even though her stuck finger caught something heavy and pulled it along with her. She realized right before the crash that it was the belt loop on the back of Becky's shorts. Her arms wrenched behind her head and she pulled Becky out of the back of the swing, sending her on a half-somersault from the top of her arc to the woodchips below. The woodchips muted the crash but the scream announced her mistake.

"Becky!" yelled her mom. She and Samantha came running as Becky sat up with tears in her eyes and a trickle of blood on her elbow.

"My head!" she yelled. "She tried to kill me!

"I'm sorry! I didn't! It was a mistake. My finger. It got caught!"

"You tried to kill me!"

"It's okay, settle down," said Becky's mom. "Come here." She picked her daughter up by the arms and examined her. She turned around to Samantha. "I'm sorry, but I should probably get her home."

"You tried to kill me!" yelled Becky again.

Emma sniffled and failed to hold back tears. "I'm sorry."

"Sorry isn't good enough!" Becky pulled away from her mom and walked back toward their car.

Samantha squeezed Emma's shoulder. "You okay, sweetie?"

"It was an accident," she said. Tears rolled down her cheeks. Her breath was choppy. "I know it was." Samantha sighed. "Come on. Let's go home."

They drove in silence. Emma wasn't thinking about the beautiful weather anymore. She walked toward her room as soon as they got back into the apartment.

"Hey, Emma?"

She turned toward her mom but kept her eyes on the floor.

"Never mind," she said through a heavy breath. "I'm going to hop in the shower."

Emma nodded and retreated behind her bedroom door. Soon, she could hear the water running through the pipes in her walls as she took off her socks. She debated changing back into her pajamas but decided against it. Instead, she sat at the edge of her bed and looked at the wall. Nothing happened for a while and her daydreams again erased time. She could have been there for two minutes or ten, and without really thinking about it, she asked if Allen was there. Then her door opened.

"What are you doing, honey?" Samantha wore a bathrobe and her wet hair fell over her shoulders.

Emma looked between the wall and her mother. The will to lie just wasn't there.

"I'm talking to Allen," she said.

Samantha sighed. "Maybe we should get you a dog or something," she said almost to herself as she walked over to Emma's bed. She sat down next to her and looked at the wall in front of them.

"Why can't I see Allen?" she asked.

"He hides when other people come around."

"But what if I want to see him?"

"It's not up to me."

Samantha put her arm around her daughter. "Emma, I love you. You know that, right? I can't stand seeing you lonely."

"But I'm not lonely."

Samantha nodded, stood up, and put her hand on Emma's head.

"Sure," she said and walked out of the room. The door slowly clicked shut.

Emma turned back to the wall where the shadows were already commingling. She smiled as they gathered together and soon there was a shape that wasn't in the form of a person, but somehow felt like one. It pulsed rhythmically and slowly moved along the wall in a vague circular pattern.

you shouldn't be telling people about us

It didn't speak out loud—it was more like a ringing in her head.

"I know, but I don't want her to feel bad." Emma spoke quietly, just above a whisper.

me neither. but people are afraid of what they cannot understand

"Maybe she could."

not everyone is as open-minded as you would like to believe, Emma

She nodded.

The sun dimmed to a soft yellow through the blinds covering David's window. He was closing in on his third day without sleep.

He made it pretty close to forty hours once in college when he went on a road trip with his roommate, but then he fell asleep as soon as he sat on a couch waiting for a food delivery. He woke up six hours later to a cold pizza sitting outside his door. But now, he was close to sixty hours and his muscles felt like they were lined with gelatin. The drawing sat face up on the coffee table. There had been a short runner's high after it was completed, but now he was drained. Physically and mentally. His movements were sluggish, his thoughts equally so, and he thought he had a pretty good chance at sleep.

The shadows on the walls of the bedroom had mostly taken over. He looked at the lamp on the nightstand on his side of the bed, then over to the forsaken side with her lamp sitting unused. He couldn't help but imagine her name on everything in the apartment. He sat on the bed and ran a hand through his hair. It felt good. Almost as good as when she used to do it.

They had a fight. Not a huge one, but definitely something that required a cooling off period. He had either forgotten to do something or had done something wrong. He couldn't exactly remember. Both seemed to happen a lot. Being forgetful makes it seem like you don't care, although he argued that sometimes you can't help simply being dumb. Self-deprecation was usually a good way to jolt Fiona out of a bad mood.

They had each taken a couple days off from work and rented a house out in the national forest a couple hours away. It was her birthday, which he worried would complicate the engagement, but he figured there was nothing wrong with piling on reasons to celebrate a day. The house smelled weird. So did the furniture. It seemed like the owner wanted to exude a royal aura with elegant patterns on both the couches and wallpaper. Medieval sconces lined the hallways and he and Fiona joked about the patterns on the walls moving around and the small busts of Civil War generals turning their heads as they walked past. Fiona was upstairs while David juggled post-fight nerves and pre-engagement jitters. The ring box protruded grotesquely from his pocket, but he figured her attention would be focused on her anger.

"Fi?" he said as he crept up the stairs.

"What." It wasn't a question.

"Hey." He breached the top of the stairs and smiled at her. She sat on the bed, on top of the covers, and looked at him with squinted eyes. "It's no secret. I'm an idiot."

"You can say that again."

"That being said, I don't think you can blame me for it anymore."

"Oh yeah?" She turned her head toward him. "And why not?"

"Because if we both know I'm an idiot, then you can't expect me to act in any other way."

She opened her mouth but nothing came out.

"And isn't expecting me to act any other way the actual definition of insanity?"

"Wait, are you calling me insane?"

David sat on the corner of the bed. Her body language didn't soften but her face did. "I'm not calling anybody anything. It's one of those questions you have to ask yourself. It's a chance for introspection."

She smiled and looked away.

"God, you are so dumb."

She looked back a moment later and David had the ring box in his hand. Her eyes shot open.

"I'm sick of calling you my girlfriend," he said as he opened the box.

David sat back on the bed in the empty bedroom with the sun pretty much gone. He smiled and thought of Fiona grabbing the ring box from his hand. He had a whole speech he was going to give her that night, but she could always finish his sentences for him. She said it was because he was predictable. He said it was because she was a mutant.

But that was all gone.

He sighed. He threw his shirt on the ground and kicked off his pants. It wasn't too hot that day, but it was still summer. The blankets were purely for decoration until autumn. He squirmed up to the pillow and closed his eyes. It finally didn't feel like he was forcing them shut. Soon, he felt himself melting into the pillow. His limbs started to tingle and the world around him faded. And then a fire truck drove past while blasting the horn.

David cracked open an eye and watched the flashing red lights bounce off his walls as the truck drove past. He was just about to fade back into the growing fog of sleep when he saw something on the other side of the room. His other eye slowly opened and he focused on the figure he had seen the previous night. This time, however, it didn't disappear.

His heart raced and adrenaline filled him with electricity. He didn't move. He studied the figure and tried to talk himself out what he thought he saw. It was the shape of a person. Long hair. About Fiona's height. About Fiona's weight. And even in this obscured state, more familiar than it should have been. He briefly wondered if he had fallen asleep and was simply dreaming. He then wondered if the lack of sleep had finally sprouted a vivid hallucination. Everything seemed too real. Everything else was too normal. He ventured a hand toward the nightstand and the figure remained. He gripped the lamp, felt for the switch, and took a deep breath. His heart thudded into the mattress below as he prepared himself to both fend off and compose an attack. He counted to three and clicked the light.

His first reaction was to jump backwards, but since he was lying down the closest he could get was to violently roll away. He landed on the opposite side of the bed and knelt, resting his arms on the mattress. Mouth open, eyes wide, heart pounding, he stared at the figure that refused to disappear this. She wore the same blue jeans and thin black long-sleeve shirt as the last night he saw her. Except now, they were dirty and torn with bloodstains. A trickle of blood ran down the side of her head and her hair looked like a wig. Her mouth hung slightly open and he could see she was missing a tooth. Her eyes focused on him, but they didn't blink. She made no noise and stayed as still as a mannequin.

"What?" David screamed. Both a question to her and the surrounding universe. "What is it?" He took another step backwards and banged into the opposite nightstand, her nightstand, and fell. He knocked over the lamp and table on his way down and screamed again as he hit the ground. He quickly jumped to his feet and found himself alone in the room. "What?" he yelled again.

He climbed over the bed and scanned the room. Nothing out of the ordinary. He yelled again and walked into the living room.

He turned on all the lights and paced between the coffee table and the TV. The sketchbook looked up at him.

"Am I going crazy?" he asked himself out loud. He needed to call Michael.

He stomped back into the bedroom and fished his phone from the pocket of his pants. His finger hovered over the call button when he saw the notification in the bottom corner next to the cartoon envelope. An email.

"Oh Jesus," he said to himself. He glanced back to the corner where he had just seen his dead fiancé, bit his lip, and shook his head. He hesitated for a moment before he clicked on it and found another message from no sender.

The future is everywhere

"What the hell does that mean?" he yelled at the phone in his hand.

"So, I heard you, uh, went to the park today," said Connor. Emma nodded. "For a little while."

The three of them sat in the living room, Connor and Emma on the couch, Samantha in the chair beside them.

"I hate this movie," said Samantha.

"Me too," said Emma.

"What's not to like?"

"The fighting," said Samantha.

"Oh come on. That's only a little part of it. It's not really a movie about boxing."

"It's about a boxer." Samantha crossed one leg over the other, rested her chin in her hand, and looked at him.

"It's about a man. Who boxes. But who's really trying to learn how to love."

Samantha laughed. "Oh come on."

"Fine. We don't have to watch it. I've seen it a million times, anyway." Connor grabbed the remote and turned off the TV.

Emma yawned.

"Yeah, yeah I guess so," said Connor. "Come on, sweetie." He stood up and put out his hand to Emma. "Let's go brush our teeth."

Emma took her dad's hand and followed him. Inside the bathroom, he grabbed her toothbrush and squirted a line of toothpaste on the bristles.

"I'll finish the movie with you," she said as he handed her the toothbrush.

"Nah, it's just about bedtime anyway," he said.

"You aren't going to brush your teeth?" she asked through a mouthful of foam.

"Well it's not my bedtime."

She spat and ran her brush under the faucet. "But how do you know?"

"How do I know what?"

"That it's bedtime?"

Connor paused and exhaled sharply with a half smile. "Because it's time."

"But I thought time didn't exist," she said. She looked in the mirror as she finished brushing her teeth and saw her dad looking back at her through the reflection.

"Where did you get an idea like that?"

She shrugged and tapped the water off her brush.

"Honey, where?"

Emma looked out of the bathroom door and down the hallway to her bedroom. She wanted nothing more than to be behind that door.

"In there?" he asked. "Was it Allen?"

She looked up at her dad, not through the mirror, and saw what looked to be tears forming in his eyes. But that was impossible because her dad didn't cry. Ever. Still, she didn't want to risk it, so she said, "At school."

He nodded but his expression didn't change. "Okay. Okay Em, go get ready for bed."

She walked into her bedroom and closed the door. She listened for a moment as Connor walked into the living room where he started talking to Samantha. Emma screwed up and she knew it. She wasn't supposed to mention Allen or anything about him. Especially to her parents.

Their talks had to be a secret. Allen said so. She knew it was a bad idea but she couldn't help herself. She walked past her closet and almost reached for the doorknob, but didn't.

She heard her name through the wall but knew it wasn't meant for her. They were arguing again. It was her fault. She wished they would turn the TV back on to maybe drown themselves out. Emma turned around and sat on the edge of her bed. She wished

Allen would stop being so shy and show himself to them. It would solve so many problems, but she didn't want to make Allen do anything he didn't want to—just like how she didn't want her parents to make her do anything she didn't want to.

There was a light knock at the door and Samantha came in. "Hey, honey."

"Hi Mom."

"It's time for bed." She walked in the room as Emma crawled over the blankets. She looked around as if Emma had redecorated the whole room that afternoon. "You okay?" she finally asked.

Emma slid underneath the blankets despite the heat. "Uh-huh."

"Okay." Samantha nodded, but seemed reluctant to leave.

Emma wanted to pull the blanket over her head. Her mom looked at her like a toy she knew she couldn't fix, and it made Emma want to cry.

"You want me to leave the light on?" she asked.

"That's okay."

"Okay. Goodnight."

"Goodnight, Mom."

Samantha flicked off the light before slowly closing the bedroom door. Emma decided to leave the lamp off.

Even without the overhead light, the room was never really dark. The streetlight outside cast an orange glow throughout the room even when the curtain was pulled shut. Vague shadows stretched around her walls but none of them seemed to be moving tonight. The window was about five feet to the right of her bed and when the curtains were open, she could see the night sky from her pillow. At the window, she almost had a good view of the neighborhood around her. Being three stories up afforded a higher vantage point than the houses that surrounded them.

She heard her parents' voices through the walls again. She couldn't sleep when she knew there was an argument on the other side of her bedroom wall so she pushed the covers off and got out of bed. She walked to the window and opened the curtains.

Almost instantly, the voices behind her went silent. In fact, everything seemed to go silent. She looked out her window as the snowflakes flew past. The orange streetlight reflected off them and they resembled little lights tumbling through the breeze. There was no chill; her room was just as warm as it had been every summer night so far. The snowflakes disappeared as soon as they touched the ground, or the parked cars, or her window, but they left a drop of moisture behind. A smile grew across her face as she watched the summer flurry, and it seemed to suck not only her parents' argument, but all noise from the air. It was still. It was peaceful. It was calm.

She watched the snowfall until it dissipated a few minutes later. And when it was done, she turned around and climbed back into bed. Feeling like she was already in a dream, sleep came quick and easy.

MONDAY

Another night without sleep. David kept the lights on, all the lights on, even after the sun came up. He spent the rest of the night sitting on the couch. Every creak, every noise from the street, every time a neighbor's footsteps sounded from the hallway, he jerked his head in simultaneous hope and fear of seeing Fiona. The terrible dull look in her eyes wouldn't leave him. The blood. The torn clothing. He needed to talk to her and he had his chance, but he blew it. He cursed himself for being afraid of the one person he wanted to see most.

It wasn't a hallucination. No image leftover from sleep. It was Fiona, the woman he was mere weeks away from marrying. The woman who went to get a measly box of noodles that he had foolishly forgotten and never came back. His phone sat on the coffee table in front of him, next to the sketchbook which he'd closed a few hours before. He thought about starting another drawing, but didn't want to distract himself in case she came back. He hoped he would be able to control himself a little better if there was a next time.

But he couldn't help wondering:

What if none of it was real?

"Oh shit," he said over his shoulder three weeks earlier. He stood over a pot of boiling water with a large saucepan on the burner to the right. Ground beef sprinkled with Italian seasoning and a little salt, sizzled.

Fiona sat at the table just outside the kitchen, watching the TV on the other side of the room. The news was on, but David wasn't sure which segment. "What's up?" she asked.

"Okay, so here's the deal: The water is boiling. The sauce is coming along. All I really need to do is toss in the noodles, wait a bit, add the sauce, and boom—spaghetti city."

"The problem being—" She drew out the last sound like a dial tone. "I don't have any noodles."

"You don't have any noodles."

"Right. No noodles." Their disembodied voices found each other around a corner. He could picture her sitting at the table, most likely with her feet perched over a corner, and he was sure she could picture him staring at the stove. It was all left to the imagination but their images of each other were so ingrained, blindness wouldn't have been able to stop them from slapping hands. He heard her chair squeak a bit.

"Be right back," she said.

"Wait no, it was my dumbass fault. I'll run out." He started to walk out of the kitchen, but she stopped him.

"Be right back," she repeated. The sound of the door opening and closing ended the discussion.

It was during a commercial break, a slight pause between commercials, that he heard the sirens. The sauce was done and the pot of boiling water had become a pot of hot water sitting on an inactive rear burner. It had been longer than it should have taken her to run to the store and back. The sirens crawled into his spine, sending a shiver from the base of his skull toward his hips. He flipped off the one active burner.

A minute later, he was on the sidewalk with a view of the fire truck and ambulance blocking traffic at the street corner to the left of the apartment complex. In the direction of the corner store.

He was out of breath before he started running, and then his breath left him completely when the fear, the exertion, and the yelling simultaneously drained his chest. He couldn't see her. She was under a sheet. But he could see the car sitting askew in the intersection with a shattered windshield and broken headlight. Sharon, who lived on their floor but was never more than a greeting at the mailboxes or elevator, walked up and told him. She shook her head. She said she was sorry.

He didn't see her before she left, and wouldn't see her again until three weeks later in the corner of his room. Even through the injuries and tattered clothing, in the sobering daylight of the next morning, David remembered her as beautiful.

He sat on the couch and looked at his phone. He wanted to call his brother and tell him what he saw but he was worried. Would he flip out at the late hour? Or would he strap him to a gurney and ship him to an institution? It had been hours since David saw Fiona but his heart continued to race.

David stood up and paced the living room. He wouldn't have been surprised if the green rug on the floor started to wear thin in the area between the coffee table and the TV; it had become his contemplation path. An off-hours call would hardly register on the scale at this point.

Plus, with sunlight filling the sky, it would technically be an early call instead of a ridiculously late call. That felt more acceptable.

He walked around the table and grabbed his phone before sitting down. He chanced a glance at the cartoon envelope in the corner. No emails. Relieved, he called his brother.

"David?" Michael's voice was raspy and deep.

"Yeah. Hey. I know it's early."

"What time is it?"

David looked to his window. "Sunrise?"

Michael's sigh sounded like static.

"Listen, I'm sorry for waking you. Did I wake you?"

"No, no I was just getting ready to lay out my yoga mat before my morning prayers."

"What?"

"Yes, David. Of course I was asleep."

"I haven't slept since Thursday."

"Wait, what?"

"Well, Thursday night. So I guess Friday morning, too, a little bit."

"David, that's not good."

"Well, the reason I called is I, uh, I think I need your help."

"What is it?" Michael's voice was normalizing. Hardening.

A short, nervous laugh came out before David said: "I kinda need you to tell me if I'm losing my mind."

There was a pause. "What's going on?"

"Just, uh, some stuff a little out of the ordinary."

"Three days is a long time without sleep, David. You probably just need sleep." There was a rustling sound through the phone. "I'm coming over. Don't do anything weird until I get there."

"Okay."

David set the phone on the coffee table next to the closed sketchbook. A water pipe creaked in the wall behind him and he swung his head around, but nothing was there.

Her covers were warm but she pulled them tighter as she thought about snow falling outside her window. Emma was comfortable in the world between sleep and waking. Her consciousness came to her in a slow drip and she wished she could pause it, but the sunlight coming through her window wasn't going to go away. She opened her eyes and saw the droplets from the snowflakes had disappeared. The shadows on the wall in front of her weren't stationary, but sometimes Allen just liked to move around.

"Good morning," she said. The shadows paused for a moment but didn't respond before continuing their dance. Emma could hear her parents in the kitchen but their voices weren't angry like the night before. Everything seemed safe. She pushed the blankets off and even the warm air of her bedroom felt cool compared to the heat she felt when she slept. She glanced at Allen one more time as she walked past and opened her door.

She was greeted by the sound of dry cereal hitting a bowl.

"Hey, honey," said Connor as she walked into the kitchen. "Hungry?"

"Who's not hungry in the morning?" said Samantha. She had two pieces of toast in front of her and was flipping through a magazine.

Emma sat in the chair to the right of her mom as her dad grabbed a bowl from the cabinet.

"Do you know where the word *breakfast* comes from?" he asked.

"The dictionary," said Samantha.

Emma smiled. Connor slid a bowl in front of her.

"It's one of those things that you never really think about but it seems stupidly simple once you do. Like the term *movie?*" Connor sat across from Emma and slid the box of cereal to her.

"I thought we were talking about breakfast?" asked Samantha.

"We are. Have you heard the term *talkie* before?"

"Jesus Connor. One thing at a time."

"So, a talkie was what they called movies right after silent films went out of style, right? And talkie was basically just a colloquial term for a movie where people talk. Like Australian people calling barbecue a barbie."

Samantha turned to Emma and whispered: "Is he talking about dolls now?"

"So in the way that barbie is barbecue, and talkie is something including talking, a movie is a moving picture. It moves so it's move-y. A movie."

Samantha held a piece of toast before her mouth and set it down. "Huh. That does sound pretty stupid when you put it like that."

"And breakfast," Connor continued, "is referring to the fast you take overnight. And then breaking it. Breaking the fast. Breakfast."

Emma smiled and nodded, surprised at her own interest in her dad's point. She looked to her mother who smiled in his direction. The feeling of normalcy flashed briefly in front of her, and even though she knew it was temporary, she savored it.

"I know you guys slept until basically noon today—"

"Not all of us get up with the sun like a lion on the plains, Connor," said Samantha, returning to her magazine.

"—but it looks like we actually had some rain last night. The sidewalk was damp before the sun sucked it all away."

Emma now had a full bowl of cereal in front of her. She ignored the milk and ate it dry. It had a more satisfying crunch. "It wasn't rain," she said through a full mouth.

"Oh no?" said Connor. "Did somebody take a big hose and spray down the whole road?"

"It was snow."

Connor laughed and Samantha smiled at her. She went back to her magazine and Connor got up to wash his bowl.

"Good one," he said.

"No, it was *snow*," she said again.

"Honey," Samantha put a hand on Emma's arm. "It's August. The low temp was, what, like in the seventies last night?"

"Snow only comes when the temperature's around freezing. That's quite a bit away from what it was last night," said Connor.

"It was snow." Emma put her spoon down and sat back into the wooden chair. She needed them to believe her.

Connor sat down and leaned forward. "Did you have a dream last night, Emma?"

"No!" She had spent so much time lying, covering up what she saw and knew, that she was starting to question herself. Allen was beyond their capacity. She knew that. Allen had told her and they had pretty much told her themselves. But Allen was real and it was snowing the night before. She had seen it herself. She wasn't even sleepy. And if they couldn't believe her on a simple fact like this, there was no point in telling the truth about anything anymore.

Samantha glanced at Connor before looking back at her daughter. "Emma, it wasn't snowing last night."

"Yes it was." Her heart raced and she had trouble controlling her breath. She bounced her eyes from one parent to the other, hoping one of them would nod their head and smile. Neither did.

Samantha's eyes grew moist. "Did Allen tell you it was snowing?" she asked.

"Allen wasn't there."

A sob burst from Samantha's mouth and she quickly raised a hand to cover it.

"Emma, baby, it was just a dream," said Connor.

"No, it wasn't." Emma slapped her hands on the table, her spoon clanging off the side of the bowl. Mouth open. Eyes wide.

"Connor," said Samantha. "She can't tell the difference anymore." Her eyes glistened with tears.

"Last night," he said, looking into Emma's eyes. "There was snow falling outside your window, last night."

"Yes!"

"You know it's wrong to lie to your parents, right?"

"I'm not lying!"

Connor stood up and walked to the refrigerator. He rubbed his chin with one hand and placed the other on his hip as he paced. Finally, he turned around and looked at Samantha.

"I think we should set up an appointment with Dr. Chamberlain," she said.

"Oh come on I don't think we need to be so drastic."

"Just an appointment for tomorrow. To talk. Just to talk." Now Samantha stood up and Emma felt like she disappeared. They usually tried to hide talk of the doctor. She had met him only once and he seemed more like a counselor from school than a real doctor. He didn't even wear the white coat. He seemed interested in Allen, but she didn't say much about him. Allen had told her not to. That the doctor wouldn't understand. Why would she talk about Allen if the doctor didn't understand?

Connor shook his head and Emma quietly stood up from her chair. She hated to see her parents upset, which seemed to be every day now, but she couldn't lie again. Not about this. She needed to be believed.

"I don't care. I'm setting it up. I'm calling him," said Samantha and she walked into the living room. Emma looked over her shoulder right before she walked down the hallway and saw her dad with his back to the refrigerator, arms crossed, looking at her. Despite everything that had just happened, the way they were all speaking to each other, he didn't look mad. In fact, he looked at her with a soft expression, as if he thought he should apologize. Emma knew she was the one that needed to apologize, and couldn't figure out why he was looking at her like that.

It took almost an hour, but there was finally a knock on the door. David hopped off the couch and opened it. Michael stared at him for a moment before he walked inside. "You look terrible."

"Is that your new catchphrase?" David shut the door but didn't walk further into his apartment.

Michael glanced around. "So. What's going on?"

"Okay, well." David walked past his brother and stood by the coffee table. "After the wake, or whatever you want to call it, I was sitting here in the dark—"

"Is that your sketchbook?" asked Michael.

"Huh? Oh, yeah it is."

"Did you draw yesterday? I bet it helped. Did it help?" Michael sat on the couch and flipped the cover open.

David leaned over and closed it. "So I was sitting here in the dark and I saw something out of the corner of my eye."

"I thought you were in the dark."

"I was."

"So how did you see something?"

David sighed. "I mean, it wasn't pitch black. Anyway, I saw this thing out of the corner of my eye and I thought someone was in here. Like a robber or something so I jumped up and turned on the light."

"And?"

"Nothing. No one there."

"David, that kind of stuff happens all the time. It's just your eyes playing tricks on you."

"Then, the next night, I'm in bed."

"I thought you hadn't slept for a few days?"

"Could you let me finish?" David paced his contemplation path a few times and continued. "So I see it again. In my bedroom. But again, when I flip on the light there's nothing there."

Michael nodded. "Okay."

"And then last night I'm finally about to fall asleep when a fire truck goes by. I open my eyes and there she is."

"She?"

"I reached over, flipped on the light, and Fiona's standing in the corner of the bedroom."

"Fiona? Your girlfriend?"

"Fiancé, Michael. We were almost married."

"Right. Right. Sorry," Michael said softly. Then louder: "You saw her standing there?"

"Yeah."

"Are you sure you weren't asleep?"

"I fell off my bed, okay? I screamed. I'm pretty sure I was awake."

Michael was quiet. His eyes were pointed at the floor ahead of him, but he didn't seem to actually be looking at it. He mindlessly moved his jaw and after another moment he looked up.

"You gotta get some sleep, man. How long's it been? Three days?"

"Are you listening to me? Fiona was here. More than that, I've been getting these crazy emails from nobody. I don't know what the hell is going on."

"Are you listening to yourself? You sound insane. Listen, you haven't slept. You've been under a lot of pressure. The human mind can only take so much."

David paced a few more times. His brother was right. This sounded insane. He couldn't decide if that would be good or bad news. On one hand, it would explain everything and lead toward a sensible resolution. On the other hand, he could lose Fiona all over again.

It was more than a morbid fascination—it was a chance to apologize. To connect. Even if only for one last time. But if it was nothing more than a hallucination, it needed to stop immediately. He didn't want to see what the next step was going to be. "You're right. But it's not like it's my choice to sleep or not."

Michael stood up. "Sure it is. Let's go."

"Where?"

"To get some sleeping pills."

David looked around for a reason not to leave and found none. "Okay. Yeah okay let's go."

A couple minutes later they walked outside the apartment complex. "Jesus, that thing looks like it melted," said Michael.

David looked at the dead cat next to the light pole. It wasn't a long walk to the corner store. The whoosh of the automatic doors welcomed them to air conditioning before the silence during the walk had a chance to become awkward.

"Sleeping pills?" Michael asked. The pharmacist pointed at an aisle with a revolving sunglasses display on the end.

Michael led David through the store like a babysitter. In a way, he was, and David was okay with that. He couldn't trust himself.

"I think these are habit forming," said Michael. "These are all just colorful boxes of risk." David stood next to him and glanced around the store. There was a large section of notebooks, pens, folders, and everything else a kid needs for the first day of school. He always hated going back to school, but there was a strange excitement about gathering the supplies. It felt like preparing for battle.

The back wall was a line of coolers housing generic groceries and bottled beverages. A pop song from the previous decade quietly played over the speakers. He turned his head to look back to the pharmacist but instead he saw Fiona looking at him from the next aisle.

"What?" he yelled and dropped to the ground. His heart jumped through his chest as his face burned a deep red. Why did he keep yelling that?

Michael ducked and looked quickly around the aisle. "What happened?" he asked.

"Fi—she's right over there."

Michael popped his head up and looked around.

"What? Where?" he asked.

"Next aisle. One over that way." David pointed, still on the ground.

Michael stood up, looked around, then back down to his brother.

"David. There's nothing there."

David stood up and slowly looked around.

"Okay," said Michael. He grabbed a box of sleeping pills off the shelf. "These will do. We gotta get you outta here and back home. Come on, David." Michael reached back and grabbed him by the shirt. They walked to the front, paid, and left.

"You really saw her again?" asked Michael as they walked down the sidewalk.

David nodded but kept his eyes on the sidewalk in front of them.

"Jesus." Michael shook his head and looked across the street, then back to David. "You're gonna be okay, man. I'm gonna stay with you today."

"No. No. Go to work. I just need some sleep, that's all. Just pretend I'm high or something. It's the same thing."

"No, it's not the same thing."

"It's close." David grabbed the plastic bag from Michael's hand. "I'll be fine. I'll take a couple of these and sleep for a day and a half."

"Are you sure?" They stopped walking and Michael looked up at the windows of David's apartment complex.

"Yes. Absolutely."

"You're not going to do anything too weird?"

"I'm going to go inside and go to sleep. Unless I have some weird dreams, it'll be boringly normal up there."

Michael nodded. "Okay. Okay." He quickly wrapped his arms around David, who kept his arms at his sides. "Call me if you feel like you're going to freak out or anything. Okay?"

"Yeah. I will."

Michael walked to his car and David went inside. Up the elevator, down the hall, and into his apartment. He pulled the box of sleeping pills from the plastic bag and ripped open the side. He grabbed a glass of water, popped out two pills, and drank them down. He set the rest of them on the kitchen table and promised himself not to take any more. He had seen too many overdose stories on TV.

The fog of insomnia felt a lot like a light wine drunk. Light seemed softer. His movements felt fluid. And he squinted at everything. Being this far into it, he couldn't tell what the pills were causing and what simply came from his state of mind. He didn't know how long it would take for sleep to come, so he needed to find a way to pass the time until it did. He looked at his phone on the coffee table like a challenge. Would his inbox still be empty? Could he ignore it?

The answer was no. He grabbed his phone with a shaking hand and unlocked the screen. His heart sucked further into his chest and his stomach turned to a block of ice when he saw a red number ten next to the cartoon envelope. He closed his eyes and took four deep breaths before opening it up to find a stack of messages without a sender.

linear is nothing

static world has always been time is an illusion

David clicked his phone shut. The messages didn't make sense. They didn't relate to him in any way. He tried to push the thoughts from his head. He failed.

The sketchbook. He reached forward and flipped it to the next blank page. He grabbed the pencil from the table and started making lines. He let the picture show itself to him and he soon realized he was drawing a sidewalk with a streetlight. He filled in the buildings and added bushes, but the picture lacked a focal point. And then he started drawing the cat next to the streetlight. Starting with the white tail and gray hind legs, he drew it flat. The same way it was in front of his building. But as he filled it in, he realized it was making him feel worse so he changed course. With the back half of the cat deflated, he drew the front as a healthy, living housecat. No matted fur. The gray chest with black stripes and gray legs had a lean shape. The whiskers and ears were perky and one eye was half-open as if the cat were waking up from a nap.

The email alert on his phone dinged and David paused only briefly before he continued shading the shadow of the waking cat on the sidewalk.

"But they said it wasn't real," said Emma.

Your parents are too hung up on the difference between what's real and what's not

"Huh?"

do you think an idea is real, Emma?

"Yeah." She sat cross-legged in the middle of her bed.

You can't touch an idea, can you?

"No."

just because you can't see, touch, or hear something doesn't mean it isn't real. Your parents are unable to understand this

"But it scares them. They try not to let me see that they're scared, but I see it. And that scares me."

What are you scared of?

Emma sat quietly for a moment. "What might happen."

The shadows on the wall swirled around the picture frame like a wave. Two full circles and then it stopped.

Everything and nothing simultaneously happens and doesn't happen at every point

"I don't know what that means."

Time, actions, events, no one can tell you they don't happen and you don't have to be afraid of them ending, because there is no end and no beginning

"Even the snow last night?"

that is a perfect example. They'll say it didn't happen because how could it, right?

"Right."

The bedroom door suddenly swung open.

"Who are you talking to?" asked Samantha.

Emma stared back at her mother and almost instinctively looked at the wall in front of her, but stopped herself.

Samantha looked at her daughter and then at the wall she was facing.

"Honey," she said and took a couple steps toward the bed. "Were you talking to the wall?"

"No," said Emma. She used a firm voice with the confidence of someone with nothing to hide. She was relieved she didn't need to lie. She didn't want to do that anymore.

"Don't lie to me."

"I'm not!"

Samantha looked back at her daughter. "Come on." She reached over and grabbed Emma by the arm. Emma leaned in the opposite direction but Samantha was simply too strong. She pulled her daughter off the bed. Emma scrambled to get her feet beneath herself before she fell onto the floor. Samantha continued pulling her toward the door. "Allen isn't real. There's nothing there." She pulled Emma down the hallway and into the dining room. Connor sat on the couch on the other side of the kitchen table and Emma caught his eye as they shuffled through.

"What the hell are you doing?" he asked his wife. Samantha didn't respond. She continued leading Emma through the front door and to the elevator. The doors slid shut and Samantha finally let go of her daughter's arm.

"Don't you understand? Why are you doing this to us?" Samantha held her palms up, as if asking Emma for a favor.

"I'm not doing anything that hasn't always happened," Emma said. She wanted to make her mother understand, despite Allen's warnings. And even though she didn't understand Allen's line of reasoning, she figured her mother was smarter than her and maybe she could get it. If she could appeal to her mother using Allen's words, then maybe there was a chance.

"What?" Samantha said, panicked.

The elevator reached the bottom floor and the doors opened.

"Here. Come on." Samantha grabbed her daughter's arm, but not as tight as before.

Emma followed her mother out the front door and onto the sidewalk. The sun embraced them. It would have felt nice if Emma weren't running through all the words she knew, trying to find the ones that could even come close to connecting her with her mother. Emma might not have noticed the sunshine, but she noticed the dead cat had finally been removed. At least something good had happened.

"This is real," said Samantha. She pointed to the sky, to the sidewalk, to the buildings. "These are real. This is reality, Emma. Can't you tell the difference?"

Emma opened her mouth but a voice behind her cut her off.

"What the hell are you doing?" Connor said as he walked up behind them.

Emma looked up and down the sidewalk. There was a woman walking two dogs about half a block up in one direction, and an older-looking man walking with a cane in the other. She glanced at the windows of their apartment complex and sighed when she saw most of them were open. Fighting with her parents in the apartment was bad enough, but she didn't want to do it here, in front of the whole neighborhood.

"You should have heard what she was saying to me in the elevator," said Samantha. Her voice carried down the sidewalk further than Emma wanted. "Where does she get these ideas?" Then, to Emma: "Where do you get these ideas?"

Lies were heavier than the truth, and her mouth was tired of using them all the time. She knew Samantha hated Allen. She just didn't understand why.

"Settle down. Hey, settle down," said Connor. "Let's go back inside."

"No! That's the whole problem," said Samantha. "We're always inside."

"Well, until you can stop yelling, that's where we'll be." Connor stuck his hand out to Emma, who took it.

"Fine. Fine. Go ahead and be an enabler." Samantha crossed her arms and turned away from them. She walked down the sidewalk and Emma could see her shoulders lightly bobbing.

After a few steps she turned around. "I just don't want to let you go," she said to Emma. Her eyes were red and her nose ran but her arms were still crossed.

"Let me go?" asked Emma.

Connor put his arm around his daughter and led her back inside.

The sketchbook sat closed on the coffee table in front of David. The pills seemed to have put him in a haze, which was a little redundant compared to the effects of three sleepless nights. He thought about all the places this sketchbook had been: Tucked under his arm as he walked to a friend's house only to make the same march home with the addition of a portrait; sitting on the stool in the hot summer sun listening to an array of musical genres at Bastille Day, or Summerfest, or Brady Street Days, or any of the other countless festivals. Every line acted as a memory. Each shape a thought. The sketchbook became a hive of recollections. A paper brain trapped between the cardboard skull of the cover with two new thoughts forever trapped inside.

David shook his head. It felt like it had feathers on the inside. What kind of pills did Michael get?

He couldn't be sure how long he'd been sitting on the couch. The sun was getting low. He stood up and walked into the kitchen where the bottle of pills sat next to the half-empty glass of water. He looked at the label and slid his phone from his pocket and searched "Melatonin." It didn't take more than a few lines of reading to see why he hadn't been knocked unconscious.

"An animal hormone?" he said aloud. The sound of his own voice startled him. Then after another line of reading: "That's also found in plants? He bought me plant hormones?" Michael had apparently bought David some natural, hippy sleeping pills when what he needed were horse tranquilizers. He sighed and grabbed both the bottle of pills and a glass of water. He shook the bottle like a baby rattle as he walked into the living room.

He looked down at the closed sketchbook and realized he felt the same drain he had the previous night before he saw Fiona. But now, another twenty-four hours later with a couple of pills inside of him, the thought of her seemed far away. Impossible. Surreal. He popped the top of the bottle and let the lid roll across the floor. He tipped the edge of the bottle into his mouth and let maybe five or so of them slide between his lips. Any worry about an accidental overdose disappeared as soon as he read about the plant hormones. David didn't really believe plants had hormones. It sounded a little too sentient. He swallowed the mouthful of pills with a big pull of water. He set the glass and the open bottle next to the sketchbook and stumbled into the bedroom.

The similarity to the previous night was almost unnerving. The only difference was the slight tingle in his extremities and an increased fog in his head. He seemed to be moving slower than he actually was. He swung a hand toward the light switch on the inside of the door but missed.

The room was dim. More dim than the living room. His eyes hadn't fully adjusted but muscle memory brought him to his bed. He sat down, swung his legs up, and lay back. His eyes were still open but, as soon as he became fully horizontal, the pills flooded his senses.

The familiar sensation of melting into the pillow, fusing with the bed, settled over him and he tried not to get excited that he might actually get to sleep. Cars went by outside but the sounds were muffled. A marching band could have been tuning up in the next room and it wouldn't have mattered. The room felt foggy even though his vision was clear. And now that his eyes had started adjusting to the low light, he didn't have a problem seeing Fiona in the same spot as the night before.

"Fi—" he slurred, holding out the "ee" sound. Everything felt like a dream. She wore the same blue jeans. The same black long-sleeved shirt. Her clothes had the same tatters and blood stains as they did the night before. She still had the trickle of blood running down the side of her head, the same missing tooth, and she looked at him with the same unblinking stare. The only difference was, this time, David wasn't afraid.

"Fi. Check my email." David tried to push through the fog and speak with her but there was a wall between his thoughts and his words.

"Draw me down," he thought he said, a small line of saliva leaking from the corner of his mouth. He reached out with his right hand but it was heavier than it had ever been. He knocked the lamp off the nightstand. The room grew darker. He leaned back as hard as he could. If he could just get one word out of her. If he could just say what he wanted to say instead of being too drugged, or too afraid he was hallucinating the whole thing, or too lost in a cloud of delirious exhaustion to string together a coherent sentence. But instead, he dropped his arm on the empty nightstand and lost the fight against his increasingly heavy eyelids.

The apartment was quiet for most of the day. Emma spent the afternoon with Connor but they didn't say much. Samantha was gone for a couple hours and when she finally came home, Emma went to her bedroom and tried not to listen to the arguing. She crawled onto her bed and lay on top of the covers. She closed her eyes tight and ignored whatever was happening on the wall and whatever was happening in the kitchen. Miraculously, she fell asleep.

"Emma, hey sweetie?" Her mother's voice pierced the nowhere of sleep and Emma opened her eyes to see Samantha sitting on the corner of the bed. The orange light of the streetlight shone through her window. Samantha stared at her with a fake, tight-lipped smile. Emma felt like the dog she had seen in a movie the week before where the owners decided her life had been just about long enough. She didn't think her mom was going to take her to the doctor to have some needles stop her breathing, but she felt the way she thought that would feel. "Honey, it's time for bed," said Samantha.

Emma thought it was stupid for her mom to wake her up in her bed to tell her it was time to go to bed, but she didn't say that. She sat up and followed Samantha into the bathroom where she brushed her teeth, then walked back to her bedroom and changed into her pajamas.

"You know I love you, right?" Samantha held Emma's head between her hands. They stood at the foot of the bed and Emma desperately wanted to return to her pillow.

"Yes."

"I didn't mean to yell at you today." Samantha's chin started to move but her voice didn't waver. "I'm just a little scared is all."

Emma reached forward and wrapped her arms around her mother. They stayed like that for a moment before Samantha leaned back and wiped her cheek.

"Goodnight," she said. She rubbed the top of Emma's head, turned, and walked out of the room, closing the door on her way out.

The apartment was quiet for another minute before Emma heard her parents' muffled voices again. She saw Allen swirling on the wall but didn't feel like talking. More than that, she didn't want her mother to hear her if she did.

The nap had stolen any chance of quickly falling back asleep. She lay in bed and tried to remember the first time she'd seen Allen—how this had all started.

It hadn't been long. Maybe a year and a half. Her eyes had always played tricks on her so she couldn't be sure when was the first time she'd recognized him as something more than an accident of the shadows. The first time she heard his voice, though, was something she would never forget.

It was in the winter. Snow blanketed the street outside the apartment complex. Cars along the curb disappeared beneath the white fluff and school had been canceled. Samantha and Connor both had to work so they asked Becky's mother if she could keep an eye on Emma until one of them managed to get out. Connor dropped her off on his way.

"Alright sweetie, have fun," Connor said as she climbed out of his car. She strapped her backpack over her shoulders, which was difficult with the fuzzy mittens she was wearing. She said goodbye and told her dad she loved him and watched as his car navigated the slippery streets. Large snowflakes were still falling and were forecasted to last into the afternoon. She wondered why work didn't get canceled. Becky's mom stood in the doorway.

"Come on, Emma. I've got a hot chocolate for you."

Emma went inside and set her backpack on the floor. She took off her boots and jacket and hat and mittens and walked into the kitchen. Becky sat at the table and looked at Emma like she had just kicked a puppy. Emma figured her only friend was still sleepy or something. Becky had no reason to be upset. They had just played together the week before and Emma had given her the good pencils to draw with while Emma struggled with the fading markers.

"Hi Becky," said Emma.

Becky just looked into the cup in front of her.

They sat at the table drinking hot chocolate until Becky's mom suggested they go outside and make a snowman while she took a shower. "The snow has the perfect kinda wet, not wet thing going on right now," she said. Emma smiled at Becky who just turned her head and walked to the closet. They got dressed and walked outside.

It looked cold when you were in the house but once you got bundled up and walked outside it wasn't bad.

"It's not cold," said Emma. Becky had maybe said two words since Emma first walked into the kitchen.

They worked in silence. Emma rolled a chunk of packed snow toward the side of the house where the snow was beginning to form into a drift. She reached the edge of the house and started working her way back when the first snow ball hit her in the shoulder. She smiled and looked at Becky, expecting to see another smile. Becky looked back at her with a blank stare.

"You think you're so special," she said.

Emma stopped rolling her snowman base.

"What?"

"Your dad drives you around even on snow days?"

"He had to go to work."

"And then my mom makes you hot chocolate." Becky pulled back her arm and launched another snowball. This one came a little fast and hit Emma where her hat met her forehead. She stumbled backwards a few steps and felt the sting of the snow on her skin.

"What?" repeated Emma.

Becky was walking toward her now. "You already have two parents. Both of them. That doesn't mean you can take my mom, too."

"Becky, wait." Emma held her hands in front of her but the purple mittens did nothing to stop Becky from pushing her into the snow.

"My dad loved me, too." Becky jumped on Emma's stomach and started grabbing handfuls of wet snow. She threw them with both hands into Emma's face. After a few scoops she rubbed the accumulated snow into Emma's nose, forehead, and cheeks.

The snow burned and felt like tiny razors being dragged across Emma's skin. She tried to cry out but couldn't. She was too confused. She'd find out later about the car accident that took Becky's father, but at that moment, she focused on the pain.

Emma stuck her hands in front of her, eyes closed, but didn't accomplish anything.

Finally, Becky stood up. She towered over Emma with tears in her eyes. Emma stayed in the snow as Becky walked back inside. She listened to the soft sounds of the backyard, the occasional wind gust knocking snow from a nearby tree and cars slowly navigating the slippery road, and then the back door opened and Emma's backpack flew out. Emma pushed herself up and didn't bother to dust herself off. She had snow packed along her backside but her face was the only part that was cold. The shock of Becky's attack dimmed the bright white world around her. They had argued before, but nothing physical. Not even close.

The anger in Becky's voice echoed in Emma's head as she grabbed her backpack and looked toward the house. Becky stood at the front window. She still wore her jacket and boots and stared at Emma. The small zipper directly on the back of her backpack held an emergency key to her apartment, and Emma squeezed it through the fabric of her mittens. She felt the small, hard key with relief and slung the backpack over her shoulders.

The cold sank into her coat by the time she reached her apartment half an hour later. The cold wind had mostly dried her tears. She half expected Becky's mom to come looking for her, but either she didn't look in the right place or maybe Becky had told her a convincing lie.

Whatever the case, Emma soon walked into her apartment alone. She took off her snow clothes and laid them in the kitchen. The tile floor seemed the most appropriate spot for them to dry out. Her hands were pruny and she was sure her toes inside her wet socks were as well. She walked into her bedroom and opened the closet to change clothes when a shadow jumped out of the darkness at the back of her closet. She stumbled a few steps back and watched as it slid onto the wall and swirled around for a moment. She let out an unconscious "ahh" sound that was mostly breath as her chest seized up. Her socks left moist imprints of her steps which led from the bedroom door, into the closet, and were now tracking backwards to her bed. She soon bumped into her mattress and sat down, facing the wall. Soundlessly, she heard:

my name has always been Allen

That had been the first time. But now, as her parents continued their stern discussion in the kitchen and Emma lay in bed, she ignored the shadows. Allen was her only friend and she wasn't sure if that was a good thing anymore. And then she heard the meow at the window.

Emma rolled onto her side, toward the orange light coming through her window. A gray cat sat on the fire escape on the other side of the glass. The white tail curled and uncurled lazily behind as it stared directly into her bedroom. She had heard cats and seen a couple run across the road but this was the first time one had made it up to the third floor.

She crawled out of her bed slowly so as not to frighten the cat. The conversation outside her bedroom seemed to be growing in volume but she didn't think it was loud enough to reach the fire escape. The window had always been sticky and it needed to be rocked back and forth, each side moving a half inch at a time to get it to open. The cat didn't move besides the slowly curling white tail as Emma wiggled the window up, letting in the warm night air.

"Hi," she said. She let go of the window and set her hands on the ledge. "How did you get up here?"

A loud bang came from the other side of the apartment, maybe a fist on the kitchen table or a slamming door. Emma jumped and the cat jerked its head. Her arm bumped the bottom of the window, which loosened it enough to let it fall. The cat jumped away. The window slammed hard on the ledge. Emma quickly pulled her fingers back. A loud pop from the impact of the frame was immediately followed by the clink of the shattered window pane. She took a step back and waited for her parents to burst through her door, but they must have been too busy to notice.

Heart racing, Emma took a step toward the window and marveled at the absence of glass shards on the floor. Instead, the window was traced with a hundred cracks, outlining the pieces that could have fallen but instead remained trapped together. She looked through the broken glass for the cat but it was nowhere to be found. She then looked at the broken window itself and tentatively reached a finger toward it.

Like a game of Jenga that was doomed to fail, the shards poured from the window frame as soon as her finger attempted to explore the damage. A cascade of broken glass fell across her arm before she was able to pull it back. Her whole arm grew hot.

Grab a shirt. Wrap it up.

Emma quickly grabbed a shirt from the floor and wrapped it around her damaged arm.

It's not deep

Emma looked at the shirt and saw a couple spots of blood showing through, but not many. She looked at her bedroom door and remembered how it felt to be standing in the middle of her parents as they argued about her. She imagined what would happen if she walked out there and showed them a series of cuts and figured it would be easier to tell them in the morning.

Everyone seemed calmer in the morning. Plus, just as Allen had said, the cuts weren't deep. She didn't need a doctor.

She held the t-shirt tight around her arm and climbed into bed. The glass remained on the floor beneath the broken window which didn't affect the shadows on the wall from the orange streetlight.

TUESDAY

His cheek was crusty. He brushed a hand against it and found the vaguely sticky remnants of drool. The hangover of deep sleep only lasted another moment before the image of Fiona standing over him sent lightning bolts through his head. And now, fully alert, he was finally able to recognize the noise that woke him up in the first place: A set of four hard knocks on his front door.

His bedroom was well lit by the sun that had apparently risen a few hours before. How long had he slept? Another set of knocks thundered through his door and he quickly stood up to find his legs were not as reliable as he would like them to be. He stumbled out of his bedroom still trying to clear the hazy fog of sleep from his mind. Maybe those pills were a little more effective than he thought. He paused before his door and took a deep breath. He unlocked the door and swung it open to find Emma standing in front of Connor.

"David. Hey. Listen, I have a favor to ask." He spoke quickly and sounded out of breath.

David nodded. "Yeah. Yeah, what's up?"

"We need to—me and Samantha—we have an appointment." He paused. "Okay."

"We gotta go talk to a doctor. It won't be long. But could you keep an eye on Emma here?"

David looked down at Emma who stared at the floor with her arms crossed. He'd never watched her by himself before. It was always Fiona in the lead position with David acting as more of an assistant. He looked back up to Connor and met his wide eyes. He looked worried.

"Sure. No problem. Come on, Emma." David put a hand on her shoulder and she stepped inside. Connor leaned toward David.

"It won't be too long. It's just a consultation type thing." He looked over David's shoulder. "Just keep a close eye on her, okay? Things have been a little—off—lately."

David again nodded. "Yeah. You're telling me." He followed Connor's stare behind him and saw Emma sitting on the arm of the couch and picking at a bandage on her arm. "She okay?"

"Yeah, it's nothing much. Physically I mean." Connor sighed. "We found her this morning with cuts all over her arm."

"Jesus—"

"The window in her room was all smashed. Says she saw a cat outside her window." Connor shook his head. "The cat from the sidewalk. The dead cat."

David looked back to Connor. "Wait, what?"

"I don't know, man. Something's going on with her. Whatever we're doing, it's not working. And now she's hurting herself?" He sighed again. "I think we're going to need to get some professional help. We're going to talk to our counselor now. Go over options."

"Jesus."

"Yeah." Connor put his hand on David's shoulder, thanked him, and left.

David closed the door and turned toward Emma. He walked to the couch and sat down while she stayed perched on the arm next to him. "So you saw a cat last night?" he asked.

She looked at him but didn't say anything.

"It's okay, Emma. You can tell me." After the last few days, David was willing to believe anything. He finally had a night of sleep and was eager to figure out if what he had seen was a direct result of an ill-rested mind, or if things really were as screwed up as he thought.

Corroboration from anybody, even the little girl next door, would be enough to prove to him that what he saw wasn't a hallucination. Fiona was somehow still around, and emails were appearing from nowhere.

Silently, Emma continued to pick at her bandage. There was most likely a pad or something underneath, but from the outside David could only see white gauze wrapped from her elbow to her wrist. He wondered how bad it really was.

"Can I show you something?" he asked. She looked over at him, but only briefly. David leaned forward and flipped open the sketchbook in front of him. It took a little bit but he finally found the page he was looking for. "Was this the cat you saw?" He turned the picture he had drawn the previous day toward her. Emma glanced at the picture before returning her attention to the bandage. A moment later her head jerked back and she stared at the picture.

"Is that the cat from outside?" she asked.

David nodded. "I drew it yesterday afternoon. But when I drew it, the cat was dead."

"Not anymore," she said.

David looked at the sketch, back to Emma, and stood up. "Only one way to find out." He started walking to the door when he noticed there were no footsteps behind him. He turned around. "Come on." Emma hopped off the arm of the couch. David grabbed the doorknob but heard voices in the hallway. "Hold on," he whispered. He listened as Connor and Samantha waited for the elevator. A moment later, the door dinged and their voices faded until they were cut off. "Okay let's go."

They walked into the hallway and David watched the digital number as it receded past the 1 to the B. Emma's parents were in the parking garage in the basement and would soon be pulling onto the street. "Let's take the stairs," he said. Three flights down and soon they were by the front door of the apartment complex. He slowly opened it and leaned his head outside where he saw the back of Connor's car driving away. "Come on," he said.

They stepped outside and stood beneath the streetlight that sat almost immediately outside both of their bedroom windows. The sidewalk below wasn't clean, but it was free of decaying animals. A neighbor that David recognized but never took the time to learn her name noticed them as she walked up to the door.

"Did they finally clean it up?" she asked.

David looked at Emma who cracked a smile. "Yeah, something like that," he said. Soon, they were back upstairs and in his apartment.

"Did you tell your parents about the cat?" he asked.

She nodded.

"And that's why they're going to see the doctor?"

Emma sighed and sat on the couch. "No. There's more." David wondered if Fiona had been visiting Emma, too.

"I think they got real scared when I told them about the snow."

"The what?"

She sighed. "A couple nights ago. There was snow." Then she turned to him. "Honest, there was!"

David didn't say anything as he walked around to the coffee table and flipped a page in the sketchbook. "Like that?" he asked.

Emma studied the picture and then looked up at him. She smiled. "You believe me?"

"At this point, I'd believe in Santa Claus." David put a hand to his forehead and tried to align his thoughts, but nothing made sense. He briefly wondered if he had taken too many of those pills and was actually dreaming all this. He was almost afraid to ask, but he said, "Is there anything else?"

Emma squirmed in her seat and gave him a few short glances. "Well," she said. "Mom started yelling when I told her about time."

David sat forward. "What does that mean?"

"Um, well Allen told me there was no such thing as time. That the future and the past and all that doesn't exist. I told my mom that and she got real mad."

David had been searching for a bridge. And there it was.

"Who's Allen?"

"Allen is, well I guess I don't really know. He comes to see me through the walls."

"He talks to you through the walls?"

"Well he doesn't really talk, but I hear him."

They were hearing the same source.

"Emma, listen to me." He faced her and waited until she turned toward him. "Do you know why he talks to you? What he wants?"

"Wants?" she asked. "He doesn't want anything. He just wants to help."

David sat back. How does making someone question their sanity help? And Fiona? How did she fit into all this?

Emma turned again to the bandage on her arm. "But that's why Mom and Dad fight so much."

"Emma? They're just confused. And it's not hard to see why."

Sometimes it felt to Emma like people thought she couldn't hear. Of course she had been listening as her dad spoke with David. Of course she heard him mention the idea of "professional help." And when she put that together with what her mom said the previous day about not wanting to lose her, she saw images of patients dressed in white and nurses speaking in calm tones.

David seemed to be understanding, but she wasn't sure that was enough. She wondered if he was crazy. Emma was able to accept the sketches coming to life because of her longstanding relationship with Allen. David was still getting used to the idea.

David paced the area on the opposite side of the coffee table in front of the TV. He continued asking her questions for which she didn't have answers. After starting her day in such chaos, she wasn't prepared to be the voice of reason.

Her day, much like David's, had started with a knock on her door. Her mom stuck her head inside to coax Emma from bed but stopped halfway through her morning greeting.

"Whoa, what the hell?" she said in a soft voice. Emma opened her eyes and watched her mom walk to the window and stand before the shattered glass. She turned to Emma. "What happened?"

"The window fell."

"Why was it open?"

Emma sat up and yawned. "I wanted to see the cat." She stretched and forgot about the t-shirt wrapped around her forearm.

"What's that?" Samantha took a few steps toward the bed and lightly grabbed Emma's wrist. She unwrapped the shirt and gasped. "Connor!" she yelled toward the door. Then to Emma: "What happened?"

"The window fell. I wanted to see the cat."

"Which cat?"

"The one from the sidewalk?"

"The dead one?" Connor stood in the doorway. "What happened?"

"It's not dead anymore."

Connor appeared next to Samantha and they looked at Emma's arm. The blood had dried and it looked worse than it actually was. Sure there were cuts from her wrist to her elbow, but they weren't deep and they didn't seem to be deliberate. Her parents looked at each other.

"I told you," said Samantha. "I told you something was going to happen."

"We already have the appointment with Dr. Chamberlain."

"We should take her with us."

"He said he wanted to talk to just us."

"But things have changed, Connor. Look at her." Samantha held out her daughter's arm. Her voice grew in both volume and pitch.

"Nothing is going to change in the next hour or two. Let's speak with the doctor and see what we can do."

"And what should we do with Emma? Just leave her here?" She pointed at the wall next to the closet. "Let Allen keep an eye on her?"

Connor shook his head but didn't say anything for a moment. Then: "Next door. David. He's not working right now."

Samantha looked at the opposite wall as if she could see through to check if David was home.

"She'll be fine over there. She's been there a million times."

Samantha stood up and walked back to the window. She stared at the broken glass. Emma, now with her arm back under her own control, slid backward on the bed.

"Come on," said Connor. He held a hand out to Emma "Let's get you cleaned up."

Emma looked at her father's hand and hesitated. His voice was calm and he seemed like he was trying to sound normal. Her arm was sticky from the blood and she worried she might have ruined her shirt. Just another thing for her parents to be mad about. She took her dad's hand and he led her to the bathroom.

"I mean I really thought I was losing my mind," said David. He continued pacing in front of the coffee table. She was simultaneously relieved that she told someone the truth and they didn't think she was crazy, and terrified of what would happen next. She couldn't keep her thoughts straight and listening to David was only overwhelming her. He didn't seem to need responses anyway.

"But now I gotta ask myself what Fiona wanted? Why is she here? Is it selfish of me that I've only been thinking of what I want to say to her instead of what she might want to say to me? But she had the chance! She didn't say anything. But what if she just couldn't say anything?"

Emma leaned forward and looked at the sketchbook. She studied the picture of the cat and was at first impressed by David's sheer talent. The clarity of the image was stunning. She flipped a few pages and found portraits of people she didn't recognize.

"Who is this?" she asked while pointing at a drawing of a bearded man with a pointy nose and large eyebrows. The cheekbones jutting out above the beard made him look as if he hadn't eaten in a while.

"Huh? What?" David stopped pacing and glanced over. "That's, uh—" He shook his head. "That's Chris. Guy from college."

"Have you ever drawn Fiona?"

David shook his head. "I didn't draw much when we were together."

Emma thought back to the last time she was in the apartment and Fiona was making brownies. The smell had filled the whole apartment which smelled now of cleaning products mixed with old socks.

"What if you drew her now? Making the brownies?"

The air in the apartment stood still as David stared at the sketchbook.

"You said you've never drawn her before," said Emma. "Why not now?"

David looked up. "You're right." He walked around the coffee table and sat on the couch next to Emma. He flipped past all the pictures to the first blank page and started drawing.

The apartment was quiet besides the light scraping of pencil on paper. David didn't know how much time had passed and he almost forgot he had a guest. Emma stood by the window and spent her time looking outside while David hunched over the sketchbook. Eventually, he took a deep breath and sat back.

The picture was set in the kitchen behind him. Fiona wore oven mitts and was pulling a pan from the oven while craning her head to look out from the picture. Her face was clear of blood and bruises, her clothes were crisp and clean, and her eyes smiled along with her mouth. She only made the brownies on special occasions, and once on her birthday when she had to go into work, he stayed home and tried to have them ready for her.

He soon learned that baking is one part following a recipe and one part alchemy. The brownies were flat, burnt, and terrible. Fiona never let him forget it. When they babysat Emma, Fiona would give her brownies to take with her at the end of the night. David used to joke that was why Connor and Samantha kept asking them to watch their daughter: A free night and a plate of brownies.

"It looks great," said Emma. She stood on the opposite side of the coffee table.

David nodded. He looked around the apartment and didn't see anything out of the ordinary. "Now what?" he asked.

Emma walked around the table and sat on the couch. "I guess we wait."

David wondered how long the appointment with the doctor would take. How far away was the office? Would they have to make arrangements or simply haul their daughter in? He felt like there could be a knock on the door at any moment and it dragged out the minutes to where each breath felt like an hour. He sat next to Emma hoping a drawing could summon his dead fiancé to make him dessert. The absurdity of it was not lost on him. In fact, he almost talked himself out of everything he had experienced over the last few days because when you lay it out, it was unbelievable.

But he had, in fact, seen Fiona. He believed that Emma had seen the snow and the cat.

His only proof of all this was that the shadow that apparently spoke with her in her bedroom also reached out to him. He didn't need to understand the connection, only recognize it. And here she was, sitting quietly on the couch next to him. All of the components to a machine he didn't understand had aligned and the only thing left was for whatever it was to perform its task.

But you couldn't rush it.

More time passed.

Each minute seemed like it could bring a pounding on the door followed by a straitjacket and stretcher for him and Emma both. No one besides his brother knew of his visions but that didn't matter. They would find him out. And maybe they should. Obviously nothing is happening here no matter what weird events he and the neighbor girl had experienced and they—

"Do you smell that?" asked Emma.

David quieted the storm in his head and drew in a breath through his nose. Chocolate. He slowly looked at Emma, who smiled and shrugged. David patted her knee and stood from the couch. She did the same.

He walked around the couch, toward the kitchen table, and looked around the wall to his left. Inside the nook sat the refrigerator, the sink, and the oven with the door open and a woman withdrawing a baking pan filled with fluffy, brown treats. She set the pan on the stovetop with a light bang and turned her head toward David.

He stared into Fiona's eyes and noticed that the vacant look he had seen the last few nights had been replaced by a familiar sparkle. He looked down to Emma who stood at his side. "Do you see her?" he asked.

Emma looked up and nodded. "And she's real?" she asked.

"Just as real as that cat."

Fiona looked at David with a sad smile. "Hi, David."

Her words sank into his bones. A chill ran from his feet to the top of his head and made every hair stand on end.

"I'm so sorry, Fiona," he finally managed to say. He didn't know how much time they had together. "I'm sorry," he said again. He started to hiccup and a tear formed in his eye.

Fiona stepped away from the oven and toward David. "It was always going to be like this," she said.

"What?"

"You've been thinking about the time we lost in the future, and the time we had in the past, but it's an illusion."

"I don't understand."

"We look at our lives through the prism of time, but we made that up. Time is just what we use to label something we can never really understand." She closed the gap between them and stood directly in front of him. "Life isn't linear. It's a singular state that never changes, even if we do."

David wrapped his arms around her shoulders. He could feel her, smell her; she was as real in the kitchen today as she was before she went to the store. He felt the same fuzziness as after taking the sleeping pills, but without the exhaustion. His chest felt like it would burst from the love radiating within. He couldn't control his mind or body so he tried to ignore both of them and exist in a place outside of linear time. He tried to think of this moment with Fiona again in his arms as a photograph, unable to be changed. He cried into her hair that still smelled of the coconut conditioner she bought a couple months before because she found her old one was tested on animals. He used to tell her it smelled like sunscreen.

"Your hair smells beautiful," he said through the tears.

Fiona didn't respond.

"So if the future is nowhere and everywhere," he continued, "does that mean we can stay like this forever?"

Fiona pulled back and shook her head. "It doesn't work like that." They let each other go and she walked back toward the stove to check the brownies. "You don't get it yet, but you will. One day."

There was a knock on the door.

"When?" asked David. He took a step into the kitchen.

Another knock on the door.

Fiona put her hand against David's cheek and gave him a sad smile. "Later."

The knocks became pounds. David looked back at Emma who stared at Fiona.

"Go get the door, okay Emma?" asked David.

"Go ahead, honey," said Fiona.

Emma nodded and turned around.

"I want to understand," said David.

Fiona grabbed his elbow and rubbed it with her thumb. "It's okay," she said and placed a soft kiss on his trembling lips.

Emma opened the unlocked door. Connor stood directly outside with Samantha a few steps back, her arms crossed and trying not to look directly at her daughter.

"Emma, sweetie, it's time to go."

"No!" Emma shouted. "Come talk to Fiona!"

Connor turned his head and looked at his wife. Emma watched her mom shrug and turn away.

"That's enough, Emma. Come on."

"But—"

"Nope. We have to go right now." Connor stepped inside the apartment. "Thanks David. We really appreciate—"

David walked out of the kitchen to the door. His lips curled into a slight smile.

"You okay?" asked Connor. He tilted his head up a bit. "Did you make brownies?"

David shook his head and sniffled. "No," he said. "Fiona did."

"Come on," Connor said quietly. "This is serious."

"Here. Look," said David.

Emma stood next to the open door, facing into the apartment. Her mother had walked up behind her and loosely placed her arm around Emma's shoulder. They watched together as David disappeared into the kitchen for a moment before returning with the tray of brownies.

"Do these look like something I could make?" he asked. "Do you remember the brownies I made?"

Connor hesitated. "Look, they're just brownies."

Something flickered off to the left and Emma turned her head toward the window on the other side of the couch.

"Look!" she said. She held out an arm and pointed at the gray cat with a white tail that sat just outside the window calmly licking its paws.

Connor looked back at Emma. "So?"

"That's the cat," said Emma. "From last night. From the sidewalk."

"Enough. We were supposed to do this quickly." Connor turned away from David. He took two steps and then Samantha said her first three words since the door opened:

"Oh my God." Samantha's mouth hung open and her arm slid off of Emma's shoulder.

She slowly walked into the apartment as Connor stood in the doorway. "Samantha, come on," he said.

"Come here." She spoke from the other side of the room, at the window.

"Oh for the love of—" Connor's voice gave out for a moment. Then: "What is that?"

Emma stood next to her mom as they looked to the fire escape. The cat continued preening as if nobody was around, but they were more interested in what was happening around it.

"Snow," said Samantha.

Connor's footsteps quickly came up behind them and soon all four were huddled together and looking into the snowy summer afternoon. It wasn't much more than flurries, but the snowflakes were undeniable. It was easiest to see the flakes directly outside the window, but when Emma looked over the neighborhood, she could see small blasts of white blowing along the sides of the buildings. It was as if a cloud exploded and the remnants were raining down.

Emma smiled a real smile and looked up to her parents' faces. Samantha's eyes darted back and forth as if fact checking the right side of her field of vision with her left. Connor took a series of deep breaths without blinking.

Connor turned around and dropped onto the couch. He put his hands over his eyes and leaned forward. "What the hell is going on here?" he said to himself.

Emma sat on the cushion next to him and pulled the sketchbook forward. "Look," she said.

David appeared on the other side of the coffee table. He knelt down and flipped open the book. "Okay, so I don't understand it either but here's what I know." He opened to the summer snow picture. "You see this? I drew this two days ago." Then to the picture of the cat on the sidewalk. "And this? Yesterday." And finally to the picture of Fiona in the kitchen. "And I drew this today." He looked over his left shoulder toward Samantha who was still looking out the window.

David stood up, pulled his phone from his pocket, and tapped a few things. "There's also this." He held his phone out to Samantha. "I've been getting these weird emails that weren't coming from anywhere." He looked down at Emma. "But I think I figured out who the sender was."

Samantha took the phone and read out loud: "Doing time whether in a hospital or jail won't fix anything because you can't do anything that doesn't exist." She looked at David. "What the hell does that mean?"

David shrugged. "Where were you going to take Emma?"

Connor put his hands back over his eyes and groaned. "This is too much."

"Imagine how Emma felt," David said.

Nobody spoke for a moment. Samantha moved from the window and sat next to her daughter. "Emma? Honey, have you been telling the truth this whole time?"

Emma looked at her dad on her left, who still had his hands over his face, and then to her right at her mom. A balloon of pride grew in her chest. Every lie she had told was to make things easier. It was only when she started telling the truth that she lost control.

But just like time, control is an illusion we use to stave off terror. Emma felt the truth of this idea even if she couldn't quite put it into words. As she sat between her parents on the couch with all of her secrets laid bare in front of them, the only thing she could put together was a simple two word sentence:

"Yes, Mom." The balloon in her chest burst and released a sob. Her vision blurred but she didn't need clarity to feel her father's, then her mother's hugs—becoming enveloped in their warmth.

WEDNESDAY

David didn't need sleeping pills. The previous afternoon provided enough mental strain to let him close his eyes and naturally melt into his pillow. Connor and Samantha and Emma left soon after the arrival of the tears. They broke their familial bear hug and slowly excused themselves to go next door. David sat on the couch, alone in the apartment, and absent-mindedly flipped through the sketchbook. He would occasionally glance over his shoulder toward the kitchen in hopes of seeing Fiona walk out one last time, but of course that didn't happen.

He scooped out one mouthful of the brownies, moist and delicious, before he walked the entire pan to the trash chute in the hallway. He listened to it bounce its way down the aluminum column until it finally slammed into the awaiting dumpster below. A couple minutes later, he did the same with the sketchbook. He texted his brother before lying down to let him know he hadn't jumped off the building and turned off his phone.

There were no dreams and no visits from the dead. As if traveling through time, he simply closed his eyes after sunset and opened them after sunrise. He woke up facing the same direction with his body in the exact same position. He simply turned off his power source for the evening and then powered back up. He rolled onto his back and reached his arms as far as they would go.

With his right hand, he grabbed his phone and turned it back on. Notifications lit up his screen and he first checked his email to find two messages, both with annotated senders. He knew who the text messages were from and didn't need to see what they said. The knock would come at the door soon enough. By the time it did, David was fully dressed and sitting on the couch.

"Well, you finally look like a normal person." Michael walked into the apartment. He paused. "Did you make cookies or something?"

"Someone dropped off some brownies." David closed the door but continued standing next to it.

"Where are—"

"They're gone."

Michael nodded and crossed his arms. "So, what? Did you just take the whole bottle of sleeping pills and sleep for a day and a half?"

"No, not really. I mean yeah I took some the first night, but I just needed to get some thinking out of the way."

"Oh yeah? And what genius ideas did you come up with?"

David shrugged and walked past his brother. "Forever isn't really all that long."

"What the hell does that mean?"

"Nothing. Don't worry about it." He grabbed his keys from the empty coffee table. "Should we go get some coffee?"

They walked into the hallway and as David locked the door, Connor walked out of his apartment with a plastic trash bag in his hand. David looked over.

"Hey. How's it going?"

Connor looked between David and Michael. "Good." He nodded. "Things are going good."

"Good, but strange." David finished with the lock and turned toward Connor.

"Yeah, you can say that again." He briefly looked at Michael before turning back to David. "Did you get any more emails?"

"No, not since yesterday. I think the point pretty much got across."

"I guess so. Hey, if you wanna bring over some of those brownies later, I'm sure Emma would love one."

"Sorry." David poked a thumb toward the trash chute. "I got rid of them."

Connor nodded with a slight smile. "Probably for the best."

David slapped his brother on the chest. "Alright, we should head out."

"See you around."

They got on the elevator that was already on the third floor as Connor slid the bag of garbage into the chute. Michael waited for the doors to close.

"What was that all about?"

"Nothing. I watched Emma for a little bit yesterday."

"By yourself? That doesn't seem, well, like something you'd do." David shrugged. "Sometimes necessity wins out."

A few moments later they walked out the front door into the beaming sunshine. The air was thick with humidity and David could feel sweat squeeze through his pores before the door swung shut.

"Hey, they finally picked up that disgusting cat," said Michael.

David nodded and smiled. "Yeah. Finally." They didn't start their walk to the coffee shop, instead staring at the spot of sidewalk where the cat had sat for far longer than it should have.

It seemed to David like the cat was just waiting for its second chance. And even though the chances of getting it were miniscule, patience paid off. He didn't feel responsible for the resurrection. He figured it wouldn't have happened without Emma. Sure, he drew the picture, but she was the conduit through which it came to life. He turned from the spot on the sidewalk to the building and looked up. It only took a moment for him to find Emma's window and was surprised to see her standing just inside of it. The glass was still broken but they had taped a plastic bag over it. He raised a hand and gave her a small wave, which she returned.

"You ready?" asked Michael. "Or do you want to stand in front of your apartment all day?"

David dropped his hand and looked at his brother. "Yeah let's go."

They walked down the sidewalk and David couldn't help but replay the images from the previous day in his mind. He looked above him, but not at the sun. The sky was clear and blue, with a few almost translucent clouds floating here and there.

"What are you looking at?" asked Michael.

"Nothing."

"It's not going to rain today."

David glanced at his brother before looking back up. "I'm not looking for rain."

Emma watched as David walked down the sidewalk with his brother. The glass had been swept off the floor and the plastic bag covering the exposed window pane ruffled slightly in the breeze. A light knock rattled the door.

"Yeah?" she said, turning around.

The door cracked open and Samantha said, "Can I come in?"

"Sure." Emma walked up to her bed but didn't sit down.

Samantha swung the door open and walked inside. Connor followed shortly after. "Have you seen him?"

She thought about David outside. "Who?"

Samantha nodded to the closet. "You know. Him."

"Allen?"

"Yeah." She stood a few feet from the door and Connor filed in line next to her. He didn't say anything and kept his hands in his pockets.

"No."

"It's okay, honey. You can tell us. We're not going to get mad anymore."

"He's not here. I didn't see him all day yesterday or today." Her voice dropped a little. "I think he's gone."

Samantha turned to Connor but Emma couldn't tell what it meant.

"Can you tell him we would like to speak with him? You know, if you see him?" asked Connor. He walked over to the closet and pushed open the door a little. After a quick peek, he slowly pulled the door shut.

"I don't tell him what to do."

"No, of course not." Samantha took another couple steps and sat on the bed. She turned halfway around so she could still face Emma. "School is going to be starting soon."

Emma nodded.

"Are you going to be okay?"

Emma imagined seeing the girls at recess. Everyone would be a few months older, a little stronger, tongues a little sharper. Becky seemed to have softened a little at the park the other day, but that surely changed after the swing incident. Maybe the others would soften, too. Or maybe they would use another few months of maturity against her. School felt so far away, even though it was pretty much her whole world. Summer vacation was a nice break, but it was still just a break. Her social life was anchored within the walls of that school until she was old enough to leave forever. But if she learned anything from the last few days, it was that time was, at best, relative. She thought about where she stood, next to her bed by the broken window with her parents that for once didn't seem mad. It wasn't always like this, but those times weren't now. And only now was real so when it was those times, it was also now. Everything was now, including the past bullying at school and if she had yet to disappear like Fiona—there was nothing to be afraid of.

Emma nodded. She glanced at the wall, next to Connor, and sighed at the stationary shadow.

"You wanna go get a soda?" asked Connor.

Again, Emma nodded.

They put on their shoes, walked to the elevator, and outside. The warmth of the day wrapped her up like a blanket and it was almost comforting. Both of her parents paused on the sidewalk and looked at the empty base of the light post. Emma smiled.

They walked in the same direction David and Michael had gone no more than ten minutes before. Like David, Emma looked around as they walked. She could see through windows and into apartments where people did chores, watched TV, and ate food. She wondered if Allen had started visiting one of them—if maybe everyone had something they needed help with.

She glanced forward at her parents, walking side-by-side and holding hands. It had been a long time since she had seen them do anything like that. She wanted to ask about what Dr. Chamberlain said, and where they wanted to go when they came back to David's apartment the day before. She knew she had avoided something unpleasant, but couldn't fathom what it was. But she wasn't curious enough to ruin the moment, so she didn't say anything.

They approached the corner store at the end of the block when she looked across the street and saw a cat by another apartment complex. It sat on the sidewalk watching her family and when Emma felt like they made eye contact, it stood up and turned away. It crouched for a moment before launching itself nearly ten feet to the base of the fire escape that ran along the front wall of the building. Emma laughed as she watched it secure its grip and pull itself onto the steel grating. Samantha turned her head but kept walking.

"What's so funny?"

Emma smiled and shook her head. "Nothing."

ACKNOWLEDGMENTS

Some of the stories in this collection have been published in previous versions. Huge thanks to these wonderful folks for giving these stories a first home:

Major Release - Originally published by *JMWW Journal*, March 23rd, 2022

Earplugs - Originally published by *The Emerson Review*, Volume 47

Patio - Originally published by *Drunk Monkeys*, Volume 2 Issue 1

Near the Tree Line - Originally published by *Foliate Oak Literary Magazine*, April 2019

Drowning Without Sinking - Originally published by *Scrutiny Journal*, February 21st 2017

Lucky - Originally published by *The Missing Slate*, February 20th, 2015

Feathers - Originally published by Tiny Flames Press, Spring 2019 Equinox Issue

Hopi - Originally published by *Cease, Cows*, September 21st, 2017

Rachel + Jeremy - Originally published by *Capsule Stories*, Spring 2019 Edition

I would also like to thank Lisa Kastner and everyone at Running Wild Press for bringing this thing to life, as well as Carolyn Banks for her keen editorial eye and amazing ability to make it seem like I know what I'm doing.

ABOUT
RUNNING WILD PRESS

Running Wild Press publishes stories that cross genres with great stories and writing. RIZE publishes great genre stories written by people of color and by authors who identify with other marginalized groups. Our team consists of:

Lisa Diane Kastner, Founder and Executive Editor

Joelle Mitchell, Licensing and Strategy Lead

Cody Sisco, Acquisition Editor, RIZE

Benjamin White, Acquisition Editor, Running Wild

Peter A. Wright, Acquisition Editor, Running Wild

Resa Alboher, Editor

Angela Andrews, Editor

Sandra Bush, Editor

Ashley Crantas, Editor

Rebecca Dimyan, Editor

Abigail Efird, Editor

Aimee Hardy, Editor

Henry L. Herz, Editor

Cecilia Kennedy, Editor

Barbara Lockwood, Editor

AE Williams, Editor

Scott Schultz, Editor

Rod Gilley, Editor

Kelly Ottiano, Editor

Carolyn Banks, Editor

Evangeline Estropia, Product Manager

Pulp Art Studios, Cover Design

Standout Books, Interior Design

Polgarus Studios, Interior Design

Learn more about us and our stories at
www.runningwildpublishing.com

Loved these stories and want more?
Follow us at
www.runningwildpublishing.com/rize,
www.facebook/runningwildpress,
on Twitter @lisadkastner @RunWildBooks

RUNNING WILD
RIZE

www.ingramcontent.com/pod-product-compliance
Lightning Source LLC
Chambersburg PA
CBHW060443310726
48977CB00001B/300